Teach Me How to Fly

Alberta Lampkins

A.L. Savvy Publications
P.O. Box 30203
Clarksville, TN 37040
http://alsavvypublications.com

ISBN 13: 978-0-9903805-0-4
ISBN 13: 978-0-9903805-1-1 (ebook)

Cover design: WWW.MICHAHDSGNS.COM

A.L. Savvy Publications can bring Alberta Lampkins to your live event. For more information or to book an event, contact A.L. Savvy Publications at 931-257-8530 or email Alberta Lampkins at Alberta@alsavvypublications.com or visit the website at http://alsavvypublications.com.

CONTENTS

ACKNOWLEDGMENTS

With Much Love

First and foremost, I would like to thank our awesome Creator for allowing me the opportunity to follow my heart and write my story. There were moments when I doubted if I should keep moving forward with this publication and after each line, that still voice within said *this is your story, keep writing*! Self-doubt is destructive, however, when you have a strong support system, like the support I have from my husband, Al, you just can't give up. My husband, along with my sister, Benita Hairston, my children, Alexis and Ahmad, my mother-in-law, Trudy Chaney and my brother, Sam Hairston, my sister, Marjorie Hairston, my friends, Zena Bell, Lakesha Parker, Netris Kinsey, Suzetta Perkins and a host of others, I could have never accomplished this writing goal. My family means the world to me and I hope my nieces and nephews, Curtis Walker, Joshua Eldridge, Alisha Ndiaye, Andre Wright, Otis Jones, Sumeka Moore, Samaria Hairston, Allysa Smith, Brittany, Courtney Hayes, Alia Brown, Dashawn Eldridge, Destiny Orr, Eve Ndiaye, Magne Ndiaye, Mia, Malachi Jones, Ari Wright, Lilliana Eldridge, Belle Eldridge, Jasmine Eldridge and any new comers, along with my aunt, Willa Mae Morris, cousin Pavaughn Morris, sister-in-law, Camille Williams, brother-in-law, Robert Cornelious, father-in-law, Clarence Chaney, step daughter, Camille, my aunt's, Geraldine and Ruth and to the entire Hairston family and anyone I may have missed, may you enjoy the story and I thank you for your love and support!

One

Heading for truth.

Startled by a voice on the train, Jocelyn jumped in her seat. The voice was loud like a noisy argument in a bar room. Jocelyn directed her eyes around the train to see if anyone noticed her frightened demeanor. No one paid her a critical view. Each traveler on train number 727 heading to Virginia from New York went about their business and paid Jocelyn Hamilton no mind.

A rather stout gentleman with salt and pepper hair and olive colored skin sat across from her with his head sunk in the New York Times Newspaper. The brown twill jacket with a piece of cloth used as decoration by each elbow stood out. His reading glasses sat atop his nose and gave him the look of intelligence. He made sure his dark chocolate leather briefcase nestled close to his legs as if he was protecting top secret information. With a carefully appraising eye, Jocelyn wondered his occupation, and if it required special education to get. Jocelyn's cloudy mirror of opinion guessed him to be a professor or a lawyer. She pondered the thought.

Her thoughts rapidly seized when the rather stout man tilted the right corner of his newspaper and gazed over at her. He gave her a semi-smile and a head nod. In return, Jocelyn smiled and nodded. After their condensed, but cordial exchange, the gentleman shook his New York Times back in place. Within seconds, he was again hidden behind the words and buried in his newspaper like a mouse in cheese.

A young man sitting alone captured Jocelyn's interest. She guessed his age to be about seventeen years old. His head bobbed up and down and side to side with Monster Beats by Dre headphones strategically placed over his ears. The music must have been like the moon walk dancing through his mind, the way he swayed in rhythm to the beats. The New York Knicks cap he wore and the black backpack with the Knicks team logo aptly suggested he was a fan of the basketball league.

With affectionate approval, Jocelyn chuckled. The Knicks regalia the young man wore reminded Jocelyn of her husband Vernon. Next to Spike Lee being the New York Knicks' most devoted fan, Vernon was probably a close second. Despite the New York Knicks having a not so good season, Vernon continued his position as a dedicated fan.

The thought of Vernon and his devotion to the Knicks gave Jocelyn a "feel good moment" and a laugh. Vernon wanted to come along with Jocelyn to Virginia, however, he felt this was a trip better left for Jocelyn alone.

Jocelyn heard that voice again. The voice came from two seats in front of her. She stood up and pretended to search through her Louis Vuitton leather carryon bag. A compelling force enticed her to see who the person was behind the voice. With covert curiosity and an accusing glance, she turned in the direction of the verbal chatter.

It was the voice of a middle aged man with beige skin and a combative tone.

"I am not paying another penny for the sorry paint job you did!"

"Oh yeah, Sue me!" the guy shouted.

The beige skin man had no problem sharing his conversation with the other passengers. He looked as if he dared anyone to say anything to him about his rude tone of voice. As he proceeded to yell, his face turned redder after every other word he uttered.

I hope he powers his phone off after that conversation. Who wants to listen to that on the train? A bit of irritation cornered a section of Jocelyn's mind.

Jocelyn shook her head and lost interest in the conversation. She decided to tune out the man with the loud voice. She had too many other things on her mind. Like finding the story behind the phone call she received after the death of her mother. The phone call which has led her to travel to her mother's hometown of Martinsville, Virginia, to meet Ms. Janie Ruth. Ms. Janie Ruth, the one person with the answers about her mother's past. Jocelyn's attention also reveled on adjusting to life as the wife of a retired Army Sergeant Major and why her friend Angel Medina appeared a bit apprehensive about her past.

Jocelyn sat back down in her seat. Before getting comfortable, she pulled out her makeup compact with the attached mirror from her bag. She dabbed a coat of light brown pressed powder over her face to freshen up her look. Jocelyn threw a glance in the mirror. She wanted to make sure she evenly concealed what she believed to be imperfections on her face.

For a forty-five year old married woman with two fully grown children, Jocelyn was still beautiful. She had been a size eight for a while, then a size ten, then size twelve. When she headed towards a size fourteen, she changed her eating habits. She started walking, working out at the gym and the size ten she wore now fit her well.

Jocelyn's hairstyle resembled a work of art. Her short bob cut always showed care with neatly trimmed edges and a healthy full body. The hints of toffee colored highlights made her selection of a hairstyle more visible and prominent. Waxed eyebrows added a necessary finish to compliment Jocelyn's questionable self-esteem about her face.

Thank goodness for waxing! Jocelyn thought.

Average height and curvy hips gave her a compelling combination of features. Her eyes were luminous, bright and brown like coffee beans. It was hard for Jocelyn to see her beauty on the outside. She'd rather people notice her humble heart and the light within her soul.

She stuck to basic lip colors. Rum Raison, Cinnamon Crush and Playful Plum purchased from Fashion Fair at Macy's to color her thin lips. Ever since high school, she has worn a stroke of black or dark brown eyeliner over her eyelid and under her eye. On certain occasions, she wore a little Chocolate metallic or golden chestnut eye shadow to change her facial appearance.

For the trip, Jocelyn wore a brown turtleneck sweater and a pair of Old Navy dark washed boot cut jeans. The brown leather riding boots with the strappy buckle around the ankle went well with her selection. The brown wool coat with the belt that tied above her hips added a nice touch.

To a moderate degree, Jocelyn was healthy. The fruits and vegetables she ate promote good health. However, her weaknesses for Lanova's Pizza and Maple Walnut Ice Cream from the ice cream shop down by the Waterfront in her hometown of Buffalo, New York interfered with living a complete healthy lifestyle. That bit of delight always came with Jocelyn having to put a little bit more work in at the gym. Watching Jocelyn struggle to go another round on the treadmill was like being in a boxing match and praying for the bell to ring.

Love of learning, curiosity and interest in the world befit Jocelyn. Treating people fairly and believing everyone deserves a chance led her to become a Patient Advocate in the hospital care system. She worked more than twenty years as an advocate; intervening, providing aid, representing and resolving issues for her clients. Her job was to take on the burdens of dealing with doctors, insurance companies and medical issues during her clients' illnesses. Her clients ranged from newborn babies with medical concerns to older adults suffering from Alzheimer's. Helping others is a big part of who she is.

Though Jocelyn had been married for more than twenty years, she still has butterflies in her stomach for Vernon. No matter what obstacles arose, so far, they had been able to overcome them. Their life after the *Army* has begun and Jocelyn can hardly believe they made it through the thick and thin of Army life.

Two

You're in the Army now.

She was hooked and persuaded by his candor. Jocelyn became acquainted with her husband Vernon twenty-six years ago in their hometown of Buffalo, New York. The glint of his medium brown eyes still held her captive as it did of days past. Clear skies allowed the sun to cascade down and radiate warmth on a perfect July day. The day Jocelyn found her way to Humboldt Park, more commonly known as Martin Luther King, Jr. Park. She was with her friend, Christina to check out the infamous Randy Smith Basketball leagues.

Vernon observed Jocelyn from afar. A quick flame leapt in his eyes, but went unnoticed by Jocelyn. He walked over to exchange a friendly word with her friend Christina. Jocelyn still didn't sense his curious nature paying particular notice of her. Vernon knew Christina through a mutual acquaintance between his brother Trevor and Christina's niece, Trina.

Vernon wanted to set up a connection. So he made his way over to where Christina and Jocelyn were standing. His cool confidence made him believe this day was a stroke of fate.

"Hey, Christina, how are you doing?" Vernon casually said.

"I'm doing well, what have you been up to, Vernon?"

"I'm just up here checking out the games."

Christina did not want to appear rude.

"Vernon, this is my friend Jocelyn."

Jocelyn accomplished a rapid and brief smile.

"Hello," she said to be courteous.

Distracted, Jocelyn saw a girl she knew from her high school and began a conversation. Vernon talked a few minutes longer with Christina, then left. Jocelyn didn't think any more about Vernon until she went to Christina's house after the park. To Jocelyn's astonishment, something unexpected happened. Vernon called Christina to search and discover about Jocelyn. To his surprise, when he talked to Christina on the phone, she informed him that Jocelyn was there.

"Do you think she would be willing to talk to me?" Vernon asked in a taut voice.

"Hold on," Christina replied.

Christina got an exhilarant thrill out of just handing the phone to Jocelyn.

"You have a secret admirer who wants to talk to you," Christina said as she parted her lips in gentle laughter.

"Who is it?" Jocelyn questioned as her eyebrows squinted causing her face to twitch.

"Just get on the phone," Christina insisted in a pleasant tone.

"Hello," Jocelyn said with a profound quizzical look and interest in her voice.

The conversation with Vernon was pleasant and Jocelyn didn't think it to be harmful to transfer the possession of her telephone number to him.

The relationship started moving like the slow tortoise that ran the race against the hare. However, Jocelyn soon realized there was something different and unique about Vernon. He was pleasing in appearance and had the characteristics of maturity. He stood tall in posture, about 6 feet 1 inch, gracefully slender and his caramel skin illuminated like warm amber.

Vernon showed up in the Fruit belt neighborhood to meet Jocelyn at her uncle's house. She will never forget that day. He showed up in a red Adidas sweat suit, red and white Adidas shell toe sneakers and a Kango hat. He reminded Jocelyn of L.L Cool J, the hip hop recording artist. LL Cool J's song *Rock the Bells* came to mind.

That's right; I'm on the mic with the help of the bells
There's no delayin' what I'm sayin' as I'm rockin' *you well*

Rock the bells

Jocelyn's heart skipped a beat. The two spent part of the day walking around the *Fruit Belt*, and the other part walking around Vernon's downtown neighborhood in the *Town Gardens*. They made a visit to the JFK community youth center on Hickory Street. The two watched a few guys playing basketball and children playing in the park. Then they traveled back to his house to eat Saturday dinner with his family. Jocelyn's eyes filled with interest. Jocelyn and Vernon spent time becoming familiar with each other's likes, dislikes, hopes and aspirations in life.

On one memorable occasion, Jocelyn and Vernon took the NFTA bus from downtown Main Street to the Thruway Mall on Harlem Road. The couple walked and talked and shared and enjoyed each other's company.

Intriguing feelings surfaced. Jocelyn felt a sense of comfort sharing her thoughts and sentiments with Vernon that day. It felt like the word love climbed out of the dictionary and made its home in Jocelyn's heart. The conversation changed from one subject to another. It flowed from *Hip Hop* to *Spirituality*. Her face and heart changed with each turn of their talk.

Young men don't usually talk about there being a higher power guiding and protecting our lives, Jocelyn noted in her mind.

Something divine clung around her. She checked the word *Keeper* in the part of her brain that was responsible for one's thoughts and emotions. The talk simply flowed.

A positive relationship with Marie, Vernon's mother; Charles, Vernon's stepfather; Madelyn, Vernon's grandmother; Trevor, Vernon's brother; Caryn, Vernon's sister and Cali, his niece was a welcome addition. She especially felt connected with his mother Marie. Jocelyn graciously accepted the invitations to Marie to attend weekly Sunday dinners after church with the family.

However, just when the two were getting close, Vernon shared with Jocelyn that he signed up to join the Army. And he was leaving in the next month. He completed two years at Villa Maria College when he decided to put school on hold to put on warrior boots. His goal was to *be all he could be* in the Army and finish college in the mix. The soulful vibe Jocelyn thought she picked up on with Vernon quickly became questionable. She thought that maybe she was wrong about the attachment she felt towards Vernon. Creeping in the back her mind stood the chance that Vernon would go off to the Army and forget about her. She had no doubt he would succeed. Vernon's ability to make his own decisions and not be swayed by what anyone else thought was a plus for him. The look of leader shined through his deep brown eyes.

The day arrived for Vernon to leave. Jocelyn tagged along to the airport with Vernon's mother and stepfather to see Vernon off. It was a sad goodbye. Vernon's mother didn't really want him to join the Army, but she had to let him go. She had to let him be the man he was destined to be. Marie grabbed her son's hand and prayed for his safety. Marie was both proud and heavy hearted at the same time. Jocelyn wondered what their budding relationship would become during his enlistment in the Army.

After weeks of intense instruction at Fort Sill, Oklahoma, Vernon finally wrote to Jocelyn from basic training. He sent a beautiful card with a long message attached. On the outside, the card had a soldier holding one finger up pointing to the words *I have one question for you?* And on the inside, the card read: *Are you ready for me, baby?* Jocelyn burst into quiet laughter after reading the card. The message he hand wrote on the inside really deepened Jocelyn's feelings for Vernon. He wrote a great letter and at the end of the message it said:

I expect to do my time in the Army and still have you in the end.

Love, Vernon

Jocelyn, unable to speak temporarily, grabbed hold of her heart with the card in her hands. His words stirred the very core of Jocelyn's soul.

Vernon finished basic training at Fort Sill, Oklahoma and Jocelyn waited for him to return. They were married at his mother's church, Grace Tabernacle Church of God on William Street. Reverend Williams, may he rest in peace, married the couple. Vernon received his duty orders and the couple moved to Fort

Bragg, North Carolina. Two children followed, Audrey and Alex.

Vernon rose to the top, from a Private First class to a Command Sergeant Major. A Sergeant Major is the highest achievable rank of a non-commissioned officer. The rise from being a Private to becoming a Sergeant Major brought many changes in the lives of Vernon and Jocelyn.

At one point, Vernon served in combat in Afghanistan for twelve months. He returned from Afghanistan for ten months and went to war in Iraq for twelve months. He returned from Iraq for eleven months and did another combat tour in Afghanistan for fifteen months. The effects of war took a toll on Vernon and the family. Jocelyn has firsthand knowledge of this. In war, truth is often the first casualty. Combat stress is real and the effects are far-reaching.

Vernon was steadfast and allegiant to the Army. He held his position as a non-commissioned officer with distinction and honor. The words of the soldier's creed became etched in his soul like a patch sewed on to a leather jacket.

I am an American Soldier. I am a warrior and member of a team. I serve the people of the United States, and live the Army values. I will always place the mission first. I will never accept defeat. I will never quit. I will never leave a fallen comrade. I am disciplined, physically, and mentally tough. Trained and proficient in my warrior tasks and drills. I always maintain my arms, my equipment and myself. I am an expert and I am a professional. I stand ready to deploy, engage, and destroy the enemies of the United States of America in close combat. I am a guardian of freedom and the American way of life. I am an American Soldier.

Those are intense standards to live up to, in Jocelyn's opinion.

Vernon never talked much about what he endured fighting in hostile territories. That may have been part of what caused a bit of grief later in Jocelyn and Vernon's marriage. At this point, Jocelyn is just happy that after each crucial deployment, Vernon returned home. Vernon survived war and Jocelyn survived being an Army wife. Jocelyn always said that one day she would write a book titled *The Sergeant's Major Wife.* In the book, she planned to tell what life was really like being an Army wife.

Withdrawing from his position in the United States Army and retiring didn't come easy for Vernon. After much debate, Jocelyn and Vernon reached a decision. They decided to move back to their hometown of Buffalo, New York. Jocelyn gave up her career as a Patient Advocate and the couple ventured into opening a coffee house café.

Café Expressions opened in downtown Buffalo. To Jocelyn's astonishment, business has been doing well. Jocelyn's love for poetry gave the café a unique flare. If you ask Jocelyn what era she would have liked to have been a part of, she would say,

"The Harlem Renaissance Era of course!"

The idea of her dressed in a flapper ball dress, silk gloves with a costume ring on top, pearls around her neck and a feathered band around her head intrigued Jocelyn. She would have insisted upon seats in front at the Cotton Club and the Savoy. Duke Ellington, Cab Calloway, Billie Holiday and Langston

Hughes would be close friends of Jocelyn. Café Expressions décor paid tribute to some of these great artists.

With the best bistro sandwiches and coffee around, Jocelyn and Vernon made a wise choice. The idea to take a chance and open downtown succeeded. Every Wednesday and Friday night, the café hosted an *open mic* night. Poets, musicians, performing artists and comedians from miles around share in the entertainment and ambiance of the café.

Thursday night is 'Teen Night'. Youth from different communities meet at the café to express themselves through spoken word and performing art. Professional jazz musicians, authors, and other popular performers have made their way to the café and have helped to make *Café Expressions* one of the best venues in Buffalo.

Three

The Art of Friendship.

A series of short loud sounds rattled from the wheels of train. The engine hissed and Jocelyn felt a brief jerky movement on the motor coach. The sudden jerk caused her to smear her makeup. Once the train was back traveling at a constant speed, Jocelyn touched up the foundation on her face.

She closed her compact mirror and put it back in her purse. Jocelyn checked the Facebook fan page for *Café Expression* and saw that five more people liked the page and made a few polite comments. The success of the café pleased Jocelyn.

Just after that, she received a text message on her iPhone.

Hope you find all the answers you are looking for in Virginia. Hurry back! Miss you with a smiley face.
Angel.

Jocelyn shook her head and began typing her response.

I don't know what I will discover in Martinsville. I would rather know the truth than to keep wondering. Miss you too! By the way, don't drink too much coffee while I'm gone. I'm laughing out loud with a smiley face. Love, Jocelyn.

I have already had five cups! Angel replied with a matter of fact response to Jocelyn.

Jocelyn decided to leave the conversation on that note.

For some reason, Jocelyn had a knack for meeting new people and making friends. Jocelyn called it her *gift* from God. She had a way of looking beyond what is seen by the natural eye and discovering the fabric and layers of the human heart. Jocelyn believed something can be learned from each person she meets. Therefore, she values her friendships and the people she feels a connection to/with. So it was with meeting Angel. Angel Catalina Medina, a fashion clothing designer was one of the first patrons of *Café Expressions*. She and Jocelyn had an instant vibe with one another. The coffee shop was walking distance from where Angel worked as a freelance clothing designer. The thought of having a coffee shop close thrilled Angel. She'd expressed her gratitude for opening the café to Jocelyn and Vernon profusely.

"I can't thank you enough for opening the café in this spot. You don't know how much I love a great cup of coffee." Angel was serious about her declaration.

Vernon thought Angel went a bit overboard with the gratitude, but Jocelyn felt that her appreciation was heartfelt. However, when Angel began frequenting the café for a cup of java before she went to work in the morning, a cup of Joe after she ate lunch and a cup of espresso before she went home, Jocelyn found it to be a little obsessive.

Jocelyn's love of learning kicked in and she made it a point to ask Angel questions about herself. Angel shared some personal information, but not much. Jocelyn believed she suppressed details. Every good investigator knows there's more to the truth than just a few facts.

Angel once told Jocelyn that she felt a warm heart and warm spirit from her. She followed the statement by saying that she did not feel that way about people too often. Angel sensed something familiar about Jocelyn, but could not quite figure out what was recognizable.

Over time, Jocelyn and Angel became admirable friends at the café and outside the café. Angel gave moral support and encouragement to Jocelyn and vice versa. She attended most *open mic* nights and any happenings the café had going on. If the events were positive for both the café and the community, Angel showed up.

One day Jocelyn finally got the notion to ask.

"Why do you drink so much coffee in a day? I mean, I appreciate the business and the friendship but, eight or nine cups of coffee a day are a lot for a person to drink." Angel held a stony expression for a moment.

"Eight, sometimes nine or ten cups of coffee a day is not a lot!" Angel came back to herself and responded with a matter-of-fact attitude.

Jocelyn pursed her lips and slightly raised her eyebrows.

"Okay, if you say so, friend." Jocelyn posed a skeptical suspension of judgment.

Angel sat back in the coffee booth at the café, relaxed her body and sighed.

"Coffee helps keep me sane."

"Besides…well. Never mind." Angel shook in her seat and reached for a cup of coffee.

We become aware of the void only as we attempt to fill it. What deep wounds ever close without a scar? Jocelyn's work as an advocate caused her to know that unresolved issues in a person's life can sometimes be harmful.

Jocelyn knew in her mind that Angel's coffee addiction had a more profound and deep meaning. Jocelyn looked at Angel and saw pain in her eyes. She concluded that when Angel was ready to share her story, she would.

The real art of friendship is not only saying the right thing at the right time, but to leave unsaid the wrong thing at the most tempting moment.

Maybe one day, Angel will share her story. Maybe, Jocelyn thought. For this moment, Jocelyn simply cherished being in a state of friendship with Angel.

...

Angel giggled at the text from Jocelyn. She had grown fond of Jocelyn as a friend, rare for her. Maybe in part because Jocelyn was like the big sister she never had or maybe Angel admired Jocelyn's freedom of spirit and soul. However, it wasn't just those two reasons, Angel felt as if she somehow knew Jocelyn. How could she know her? Her first time meeting Jocelyn happened the day she walked in *Café Expressions*. Still, she couldn't help the sentiment.

At times, Angel felt like a trapped bird caught in a cage. She hid her past so deep that she believed she had no life before moving to Buffalo. Angel supported Jocelyn traveling to her mother's hometown of Martinsville, Virginia. However, she did not think it necessary to dig up the past. She couldn't understand why Jocelyn felt such a need to do so.

Some things in life are just better left undiscovered! Angel's opinion stimulated from something much deeper. Angel felt that the stories Jocelyn shared about her life were kind of great. Why Jocelyn went searching for a different account puzzled Angel.

A person does not have to tell you everything about their life. It does not matter, mother or not. People have a right to secrets, right?

Angel thought about that day in the coffee shop when she and Jocelyn talked. She almost told Jocelyn her story, but ruled against it. For years she has stayed quiet and kept the memories of the past to herself. She couldn't even gather the nerve to talk to her mother about her restless nights and nightmares of her long ago life.

Angel felt that her life, in many ways, was in direct contrast to Jocelyn's. Jocelyn never seemed to meet a stranger and always had a positive outlook on life. Jocelyn genuinely trusted people and had faith that everything happens in a person's life for a reason.

To Angel, everyone was a stranger and she trusted no one besides her mother. Cecelia, Angel's mother, lived in Oak Manor, a senior living apartment complex on Main Street in Buffalo. Angel visited her mother regularly. Susan, Angel's aunt on her mother's side, passed away of a brain tumor years ago. No other family lived in Buffalo.

The only other person Angel considered "like" a great aunt to her was Ms. Kay. Ms. Kay lived at Oak Manor and always looked out for Angel's mother. Ms. Kay never let the other residents take advantage of Cecelia. Angel appreciated Ms. Kay looking out for her mother. Ms. Kay treated Angel kindly, never asked her any intruding questions and understood the "everything doesn't have to be told" rule. Ms. Kay called Angel, "Cat," short for Angel's middle name of Catalina. She would be the only one Angel allowed to call her by the name "Cat."

A few years ago, Ms. Kay's health began to decline. Her family moved her to North Carolina with the daughter she called *Peaches*. Ms. Kay planned to have one of her children give she and Cecelia her forwarding address. However, they never heard from Ms. Kay again. Angel had hoped to keep in touch with Ms. Kay.

Angel often wished she could see the world through a different lens. Like through Jocelyn's eyes, but she just couldn't get over the things she'd seen in her lifetime. Whenever anyone got too close to her, she found an excuse to push them away or they left, like Ms. Kay. For some reason, her friendship with Jocelyn felt safe. Even so, she was not ready to uncover what she desperately tries to hide.

Some people drink alcohol, some smoke, some do drugs, some people cut and others use different forms of addictive behavior to hide behind pain. Coffee was Angel's vice. There were nights when she did not want to fall asleep, for fear she would relive the day she left the Bronx and moved to Buffalo. Caffeine kept her awake. Coffee allowed her to function normally, well, normal for Angel. Two cups became three, three became four, and four became five and so on.

Angel trembled at the thought of sharing her story and quickly made a mad dash for a cup of coffee.

ALBERTA LAMPKINS

Four

The life she thought she knew.

Why did Jocelyn feel the need to find the truth? She had a pretty normal life. Why not just leave the past, the past? Would Jocelyn's life be any different if her mother told her the real story? Here is Jocelyn's life story, as she knew it to be true.

The warmth of the July sun welcomed Western New Yorkers in nineteen sixty eight. The year Jocelyn arrived in the world; the last of five children born to Henry and Katie Harris. Hard to believe, but Henry, fifty-eight years old and Katie, forty, added one more child to their family when Jocelyn made her appearance. Jocelyn's conception was unexpected. Her parents believed that her brother, who preceded her by a year, would be the last of the Harris children. God had other plans. Destiny took control and along came Jocelyn. Due to complications during delivery, Jocelyn showed up by way of a caesarian section.

After Jocelyn's birth, Katie received notice she would not bring into being any other children. The doctor performed a peripartum hysterectomy, which actually saved her life. Though traumatic, she managed to be content with knowing she would only have her five children: Alexandra, Marian, Bonnie, Henry Jr. and Jocelyn.

Jocelyn's father, Henry Harris Sr., was born in West Virginia in the vibrant year of nineteen-ten. His age added up to be eighteen years older than Katie. As the third of twelve children born to Donald and Elaina Harris, Henry was no stranger to a large family. His honey colored skin, high stature and lean body build heightened his handsome features. Known to be dependable, Henry helped care for all of his brothers and sisters. The Harris family lived in Bluefield, West Virginia for years before moving to a small farm right outside of Martinsville, Virginia.

Donald Harris, Jocelyn's paternal grandfather, worked in the coal mines in West Virginia. When her father Henry and Henry's brothers came of age, they also worked as coal miners. Mining was considered a dark, dirty and dangerous profession. It is a labor-intensive industry, but the Harris men stood proud. They did the work to help keep the family together. Elaina, Jocelyn's grandmother, worked as a seamstress part time to add extra money to the household. The family did not have a great amount of wealth, but they were able to meet their basic needs. They cared for each other with love and respect.

During World War II, Henry received notice of his draft in the United States Army. The draft notice confirmed his assignment to serve with the 163rd Laundry Company as a general carpenter. He left to serve his country in October of 1943 from Fort Harrison, Indiana. Heroically, he fought in battle with valor and distinction.

Henry was honorably discharged in November of 1945 from Fort Dix, New Jersey. Henry fought in the war in Ardennes, Belgium, Central Europe, Normandy, France, Northern France and Rhineland, Germany. He earned the European-African-Middle Eastern Campaign Medal with one silver service star; World War II Victory Medal; Honorable Service Lapel Button WWII; and the Sharpshooter Badge with Rifle bar.

Henry traveled around the country for a short time after he returned home from war. Eventually, he made his way back to West Virginia, then to Martinsville, Virginia. He lived a bountiful life before meeting Katie.

Katie was born in Martinsville, Virginia in 1928 to Alice and Walter Redding. Katie, the oldest of three girls, loved her two younger sisters, Jocelyn (whom Jocelyn is named after) and Lynette. Katie's father, Walter, owned and operated a cab stand. Walter worked as a chauffeur for years until he saved up enough money to buy his own cab. It was a prideful moment for Walter. He wanted to be a good provider for his wife and three growing girls. He managed a strict home and had to be hard on all three of his beautiful girls, but harder on Katie. Likely because Katie was the oldest and needed to set the example for her two younger sisters. Katie's mother, Alice, worked as a clerk in the local department store in Martinsville. The family lived in the home with George and Hanna Harris, Alice's parents. George, a dedicated elder and minister of the church, made sure his granddaughters went to service every time the church doors opened. Jocelyn and Lynette were obedient and followed the strict rules enforced by their grandfather and parents.

Katie, born with a bit of rebellion in her, often tested the limits. Her grandmother instantly knew Katie would be a handful. From an infant, she had a mind of her own. She threw glass bottles filled with milk across the floor. Katie's grandmother, Hanna, had to give her milk in a coca cola bottle because they were heavier and tough for her to break. Hanna often protected Katie. She frequently grabbed the hand of Katie's father and grandfather to prevent them from giving Katie too many lashes. "I'll take the next lick, just leave this child alone."

According to family testimony, Katie received more whippings than the three sisters together. When Katie came to be a certain age, instead of going to church, she would sneak off with friends to the dance hall. The big bands played at the hall and Katie made herself present for the shows. Cab Calloway, Lord Price and Jimmy Lunsford were a few of the entertainers she risked punishment to see.

Growing up in such a rigid Christian environment was not easy for Katie. There were countless church sermons, bible studies, Sunday school attendances, church picnics, pastor's anniversaries, and Wednesday night prayer services. Not to mention, tent revivals. Katie felt unlike her sisters Jocelyn and Lynette, to a certain degree. Her siblings went along with the strict set of rules. Katie bent the rules.

Alice, Katie's mother, displayed a sense of self-respect and dignity. She believed in making sure her three girls were the best dressed girls in Martinsville. The girls were trained to be polite, courteous and of good manners. Education was priority. Alice went to great lengths to insure each daughter graduated and that they attended an institution of higher learning. Alice disapproved of some choices she made in her past, but let it go and focused on her girls. She felt she did what she had to for the betterment of her children.

Katie and Lynette graduated from the Kate Bitting Reynolds Hospital School of Nursing in Winston Salem, North Carolina. The nursing school and hospital opened in 1938 for the treatment of black patients and the education of black medical students. The hospital and school closed in 1970 and was torn down. Jocelyn, Katie's sister, graduated from Winston Salem State University with a teaching degree.

After all three girls received a degree, their mother Alice took ill. She was diagnosed with cancer. Surgery to remove the cancer was unsuccessful. Due to complications during the surgery, Alice succumbed to death. She passed away in the hospital where her two daughters worked as nurses. Alice's death sent Walter into a sunken feeling of gloom. He drank excessively and the alcoholic beverages he gulped became his crutch.

One evening while driving his cab under the influence of liquor, he had an accident. Walter was thrown from his cab and suffered major injuries. He lost the use of his legs. Without the use of his lower limbs he was no longer able to drive or work. The sudden death of his wife and unemployment status left him more dependent on alcohol. He caused irreparable damage to his liver. With the obstruction to his liver, his body could no longer perform as expected. Walter soon died.

The permanent loss of their parents was hard to bear for Katie, Jocelyn and Lynette. They made a solemn pledge to stick firmly together as sisters. Hanna died a few years after Alice and Walter. Katie's grandfather lived to be ninety-six years of age.

Five

One father is more than a hundred Schoolmasters.

M r. "Big Shot" is what everyone in Martinsville called Henry. He dressed well, clothed in a respectable shirt, a well refined jacket and brim hat. He gained knowledge early on how to manage his money and how to spend it sparingly. He saved and bought items he most desired and had money to spare.

Henry held tight as a visionary and believed that if he worked hard, there wasn't anything that he could not accomplish. He freely gave to his friends and family. Hence is where he got the name "Big Shot." Buying a round of drinks for his friends was a normal and carefully practiced deed. He never left out his acquaintances living in the *bottoms* that didn't have as much as he had to give. And he never asked for anything in return. No matter how many times he left

Martinsville and came back, he always made it a point to visit his friends. His friends respected his loyalty.

Being born under the Zodiac sun sign of Aries made him a natural born leader. Power driven and competitive in everything he did, he achieved success at a young age and built a good reputation. A matchless debater, it made him persuasive and passionate about causes he believed in. Enthusiasm for life came easy for him and he inspired others; even some younger than he admired his characteristics.

Putting into service the skills he learned while serving in the Army, he secured work as a brick mason and carpenter for Dr. Anderson. Dr. Anderson earned the status as a prominent and successful person in Martinsville. He served as the only doctor and pharmacist to nearly all the African Americans who lived in Henry County and the surrounding areas. His leadership and entrepreneurial spirit pushed him forward to open a drug store with an adjoining soda shop. He went on to open a bowling alley, a barber shop and a private physician office to see his patients. He hired Henry as a contractor to help build these successful venues. The people in the town of Martinsville all supported the businesses opened by Dr. Anderson.

Dr. Anderson belonged to a prestigious Baptist Church on High Street in Martinsville. He organized town meetings and gatherings to support local black business development in the area. He married a beautician; however, the couple never had children. Martinsville became a hub for sophisticated blacks and families. It was one of the only towns around that had a good share of black owned businesses.

Henry caught the entrepreneurial spirit and partnered with a good friend of his to open B&H bowling alley. Dr. Anderson founded the July Jubilee Festival. The festival attracted popular black jazz and blues artists from miles around to show off their talent. Henry took part in helping Dr. Anderson organize the event. The Jubilee Festival was the premiere highlight of black life in Martinsville.

The glimpse of a curvy woman with shapely legs, smooth skin and natural hair caught the attention of Henry. She attended the festival with a few of her friends. Henry had to go over and introduce himself to her. He was eighteen years her senior, but age was just a number because Henry was smitten by Katie.

Katie, charmed by how Henry approached her, approved of his style. The two sat at a little table in the corner of the hall and talked. Katie informed Henry she started work as a nurse for Dr. Anderson. Henry shared that he worked construction and ran a business on the side. Henry knew at that moment, Katie would be his wife.

Henry loved to travel. He told Katie stories about all the places he had been while in the Army. He also told her about the places he'd visited after he returned home. She found interest in his travel to Harlem, New York and Buffalo, New York. The stories he shared about what the north was like, fascinated Katie. She had lived in Martinsville all her life. The thought of leaving Martinsville engaged Katie's mind. Without a second thought, she agreed to pack up and leave for a new adventure with Henry. The news shocked Katie's sisters Jocelyn and Lynette.

"You are being ridiculous." Lynette turned her nose up.

"Running off to live up north with that Henry is not a good idea, Katie," Lynette insisted.

Lynette did not care too much for Henry because she had heard about his reputation as *"Mr. Big Shot."* Lynette did not want her sister hurt by Henry.

Katie's middle sister, Jocelyn chose to support her decision. In a way, Jocelyn admired Katie for taking a chance on life and doing something she wanted to do. Katie got the blessing from her grandfather George, and prepared to leave Martinsville.

ALBERTA LAMPKINS

Six

Taking a chance on love.

Henry and Katie packed up their personal belongings in Henry's 1954 Ford and headed to Harlem, New York. The couple spent two years in Harlem and moved to Buffalo, New York. Eventually, Henry's parents and siblings moved to Buffalo as well.

Buffalo thrived in steel manufacturing, rail car manufacturing, automobile production and grain storage industry. The town started around 1789 as a small trading community. Buffalo grew quickly after the opening of the Erie Canal. Buffalo has been home to many African-Americans, dating back to 1828. Home to the first electric street lights in the United States, Buffalo was a terminus point for the Underground Railroad. Many fugitives crossed the Niagara River from Buffalo to Fort Erie, Ontario

Canada to freedom. Henry and Katie believed this was the place to raise their family.

A black man could get a decent job and provide well for his family in Buffalo at that time. With Henry's experience, he had no problem finding work as a brick mason and contractor in Buffalo. Katie established work as a nurse at Millard Fillmore Hospital and soon came her first born child, Alexandra. Then along came Marian, then Bonnie.

Henry traveled around to different places, doing jobs that paid the most for his skill. With Henry in and out of town, Katie felt overwhelmed. She was caring for her three children and maintaining her job as a nurse. Soon after, her sister Jocelyn arrived from Martinsville to help out with the children.

Jocelyn taught school at School thirty-seven on Carlton Street in Buffalo. Later, she worked as a Social Worker for the Erie County Department of Social Services. Jocelyn met and married Franklin and made Buffalo her permanent home. Katie's sister, Lynette, married a Preacher's son and moved to the Washington, D.C. area.

Henry, Katie and the three girls lived in the projects on South Division Street near downtown for a short time. Henry saved up enough money to build the family a home on Cayuga Street. Henry purchased an odd shaped plot of land. He saw potential with the property. He turned that odd shaped land into a great brick home. Henry chose a pale red brick to make the home like no other on the street. The home with five bedrooms was perfect for his growing family. He completed the work in time for the birth of the next two Harris children. Henry Jr. and Jocelyn were the last of five children. Jocelyn was her aunt's namesake and she loved every minute of holding that title.

Katie's sister Jocelyn and her husband Franklin bought a house less than ten minutes away on Peach Street. The neighborhood, known as the *Fruit Belt,* had streets named after different kinds of fruit - Peach Street, Grape Street, Orange Street, Lemon, Cherry and Mulberry Street. German settlers once occupied the Fruit Belt neighborhood. When they arrived, they brought with them roots from the orchards in their native land. Each street was named after the fruit orchard it housed.

Major steel production, automobile manufacturing and other plants closed in Buffalo. The German settlers and other residents moved out of the city to the suburbs and other surrounding areas. They left the community and took their businesses with them. The Fruit Belt became a hub for middle class African Americans. However, as the economy suffered so did the Fruit Belt. Middle income became low income.

With Katie working primarily night shifts at the hospital and Alexandra, Marian and Bonnie in school fulltime, Henry Jr. and Jocelyn got to spend time with their father. He would often pack them a lunch and take Henry Jr. and Jocelyn to different worksites around the city with him. He taught them how to lay and bind the bricks with mortar. Both Henry Jr. and Jocelyn found it exciting. Wherever Henry Sr. went, Jocelyn and Henry Jr. wanted to tag along. They both loved their dad.

Nine of Henry's brothers and sisters were living in Buffalo and had a strong family bond and attachment to each other. Henry and his brother Ronald worked together building houses and buildings in Buffalo. Jocelyn enjoyed when her dad got together with his siblings. Her uncle Ronald loved to *Hambone.* Jocelyn got a kick out of seeing him patting and slapping his hands across his knees, thighs and body in a rhythmic fashion. As he made the sounds with his hands, he would also sing.

"Hambone, Hambone where you been? Round the world and I'm going again."

"What you gonna do when you come back? Take a little walk by the railroad track."

"Hambone, hambone have you heard? Papa's gonna buy you a mocking bird. And if that mocking bird don't sing, Papa's gonna buy me a diamond ring" and so on.

Playing the drums was an African tradition. Slave masters stripped or banned slaves from following any of their ancestral traditions, such as playing drums. According to a theory, slaves began to use their bodies as percussion. Hamboning carried on for generations. In 1952, Red Saunders recorded the novelty hit titled,"Hambone." Red Saunders was an African American percussionist who played music ranging from jazz to blues to R&B. He played with the legendary likes of Albert Ammons, Louis Armstrong, Duke Ellington, and Woody Herman. Jocelyn, only five years old, would try to hambone along with her uncle.

Henry Sr. enjoyed playing games with his children. He would tap one of them on the head and say *"Where ya headed."* Tap them on the back and say *"When ya coming back."* Tap them on the knee and say *"Your Momma needs ya."* He always knew how to make them laugh.

Cayuga Street, a dead-end, had a friendly family atmosphere on the short road. At that time, there were about fifteen families living on the street. The families became uniquely close to one another. Everyone knew everyone on the street and the children all played together. Jocelyn's house sat at the end of the street; the last brick house on the odd shape land before the bridge. Henry made a tire swing attached to the strongest branch of the tree. The tree stood in the front yard. The swing became a source of enjoyment for all the children on the street. There would be times when the children pushed and shoved each other. They fought to get first in line to swing.

Jocelyn, Henry Jr., and Bonnie were particularly close to Sheena and Katrina. Sheena and Katrina were sisters who lived on Cayuga with their great-grandmother and great- grandfather. They became close and called each other cousins. Deanna lived with her parents and sister two houses from Sheena and Katrina. The Hawthorns, whose father was a successful minister, lived near Sheena and Katrina's house. The Gladwins lived across the street. The families were all closely connected.

The children on the street would take off the cap to the red fire hydrant that sat across from Jocelyn's house. The water gushed out. The children put on their swimming suits, shorts and swimming caps and had a ball playing in the water. They played as long as they could. That is until someone reported what they had done. It did not stop them from doing it one or two more times.

Jocelyn, Katrina and Robin, one of the Hawthorne girls, would pretend to be one of the Angels from the hit television show *Charlie's Angels*, an American crime show plotted around three ladies working as private detectives. Jocelyn, Katrina and Robin argued over who would be which Angel. They decided. Jocelyn played the role of Sabrina Duncan, the character on the show played by Kate Jackson. Katrina played Jill Munroe, the character on the show played by Farrah Fawcett. Robin played Kelly Garret, the character on the show played by Jaclyn Smith. The three solved pretend crimes happening on Cayuga Street.

The young people of Cayuga Street kept up with the latest fashions of the seventies. Little flat shoes made of plastic in assorted colors they called "Jelly" shoes. Flared jeans, they called "Bell Bottoms" and "Tube Tops" made of elastic stretched cloth in flowered, striped and solid colors. Gaucho pants, penny loafers and Chinese slippers they called "baby doll" shoes were also popular among the preteens.

Summer nights, Jocelyn, her parents, brother and sisters would sit out on the porch and play games. Henry Sr. would bring one of the televisions the family owned outside and the family would watch a show on the porch. Henry Sr. enjoyed watching the popular television show *The Waltons*. The family would watch the Waltons together as well as *Sanford and Son*, featuring Redd Fox. The show *Good Times* starring Jimmie Walker was another family favorite. Jocelyn proudly wore her red tee shirt with the picture of J.J from the show, and the famous quote from J.J pressed on it, *Dyn-o-Myte!*

Katie teased Henry Sr. about having fondness for the actress, Lola Falana. She was a popular black singer, dancer and actress from the sixties and seventies. Sammy Davis Jr. discovered Lola Falana while she was dancing in a night club. He gave her a featured role on his 1964 Broadway musical "Golden Boy." Later in her career she recorded under Frank Sinatra's record label. Lola Falana starred in her first film role in the film *A Man Called Adam*. Ossie Davis and Cicely Tyson starred in the film along with Lola Falana. Throughout the mid-seventies, Lola Falana made guest appearances on popular TV shows like *The Tonight Show Starring Johnny Carson, The Muppet Show, Laugh-in* and *The Flip Wilson show.*

In the midst of an urban neighborhood, the Harris family living on Cayuga street never felt underprivileged or deprived. For Henry Sr. and Katie, family was most important. Henry Sr. would always tell his children to stick together and look out for each other no matter what life brings.

Jocelyn and her siblings attended School number thirty-nine, also called Martin Luther King Jr. Multicultural Institute. The school sat across the street from Jocelyn's house. Jocelyn attended from pre-school all the way to eighth grade. Dr. Dixon, the school principal, knew most all the parents of the children who attended school thirty-nine. He had a vested interest in seeing the young brown girls and boys of his school succeed. Back then, he had permission to paddle any student that was misbehaving and Jocelyn's brother Henry Jr. had his share of paddling in those days. Jocelyn's family lived right across the street from the school, yet her brother Henry Jr. would often be late. He wanted to stay home with his father. He had to be dragged to school by his sisters each morning.

There were many great teachers at school thirty-nine. However, Jocelyn's favorite teacher of all time is Mrs. Karima Amin. Jocelyn found Mrs. Amin to be a wonderful role-model. She wore dresses and clothing made from Kente cloth and a head scarf to match. Jocelyn enjoyed listening to her act out African folktales and stories. She taught the children in her class about African culture and traditions. Lessons not found in the standard history books. Karima Amin provoked thought and gave a sense of pride to her students. She goes down in history as an awesome educator in Jocelyn's eyes.

ALBERTA LAMPKINS

Seven

More than just brick and mortar.

H enry Sr., delighted in adding or fixing up something new to their home and Jocelyn enjoyed watching him work. Since the school was located directly across from their home, during recess, Jocelyn would run to the fence and wave to her father as he worked on the house. Henry Jr. ran to the fence as well, but it was to beg his father to let him come home. Henry Jr. never liked going to school, especially if he could be home with his father. His rebellion often landed him in trouble at school and home. Henry Sr. would talk to his son, but never physically disciplined him. Katie had that responsibility of whipping Henry Jr. Henry Sr. often instigated the tango between Henry Jr. and Katie. He would jokingly advise Henry Jr. how to get out of a spanking.

"Run, boy, run. Run up under the bed, your momma can't fit up under there!"

Henry Jr. took it as sound advice and did exactly as his father said. He ran under the bed. Most times, Katie just gave up and Henry Jr. got away with murder. Well, he was the only boy.

Heavier than she was before she met Henry Sr., Katie's primary focus became her children and not herself; making sure they had what they needed and often times what they wanted. She never spent much on herself, she wore her hair in the same style, wore the same style clothes and she never wore make-up. Her best friend was her sister, Jocelyn. She kept close phone contact with her sister Lynette in Maryland as well. Her children were simply her life.

Alexandra, the oldest of the five children was by far the most eccentric. She crowned in as the hip one. The latest eight track tapes or music records by the most popular artists of the 70's established a home with Alexandra. If she was not playing a tape or listening to one of her records, she would be listening to WBLK, Buffalo's most popular radio station. At times, pre-occupied with her own thoughts, she was "closed" off from the family. Alexandra kind of accepted whatever life gave her; making her introverted in a way.

Beauty didn't require her to audition; she had that part nailed down. Her long black hair that reached past her shoulders complimented her small frame. Decorated with fake eyelashes, big hoop earrings, halter tops, cork heeled sandals and eye shadow that matched each outfit described her style in the 70's. She was ten years older than Jocelyn. And she admired everything about her sister. She would sneak upstairs, slide her hands across the beads Alexandra had hung across the door and enter Alexandra's room. Alexandra's room filled a young girl with interest in fashion. The clothes, the make-up, the shoes along with the music gave Jocelyn lots of stuff to get into.

Jocelyn put on Alexandra's platform heels, her make-up and sang Natalie Cole's song *Our Love*.
"Our Love will stand tall as a tree. Our Love will be for the whole world to see. Our Loveeeee."

Jocelyn sung out of tune, with Alexandra's hairbrush as her microphone. Alexandra caught her in her room and fussed.

"I told you not to be getting in my stuff."

Kind of a neat freak, Alexandra went about putting everything Jocelyn messed with back in its place.

"You have all those Barbie dolls and games to play with and you up in my stuff. Now sit down here so I can fix your hair."

Being the oldest made her naturally responsible for helping to care for her siblings. Her primary duty was to wash and straighten Jocelyn, Bonnie and Marian's hair. Alexandra had no mercy when it came to detangling their hair and straightening it out. She sat them on the floor between her knees. She pulled and yanked their heads until their hair was manageable. She got out the hot comb and straightened a section of hair at a time. The sizzle of the hot comb going through Jocelyn's hair always made her nervous. Alexandra hailed as being skilled;

she never once burned any of them with the straightening comb.

As Alexandra got older, she wanted to be more independent. She often pushed the limits with her father. At times, Alexandra spent hours in her room alone; listening to her music and sort of, in her own world. She started smoking pot. Henry Sr. found out. She also got caught a few times drinking beer. Katie always defended Alexandra. She let her go stay with Aunt Jocelyn when she needed time away from the house. Staying out of the spotlight made Alexandra modest. She never really regarded herself as special, though to Jocelyn her sister was special.

Marian also had the responsibility of helping to care for her siblings. Alexandra and Marian often bumped heads. She did Jocelyn's hair along with Bonnie's during the time Alexandra spent over her Aunt Jocelyn's house. Marian always did their hair in one style. She put a part down the middle of their head, and two French braids along the side. Marian sealed the end of the braids with a rubber band. That was about all she was going to do. She didn't have the time or patience for any fancy hair styles. Marian had no problem expressing how she felt about any subject.

She was a 'brick house', with hair that went past her shoulders and a shapely stature. Bold, candid and outspoken are characteristics that clearly define Marian. Henry Sr. felt duty bound to be strict on all of his girls, particularly Alexandra and Marian. When Marian became of age to date, Henry Sr. would have Jocelyn and Henry Jr. sit in the room with Marian and her boyfriend. The two spies reported anything they saw suspicious. Marian hated that she had no privacy; however, she had no other choice but to respect the rules of the house.

Peddling her frustrations out on cloth, Marian was fierce with a sewing machine. Designing clothes was second nature to her. Often times when Bonnie, Jocelyn and Henry Jr. were outside playing, Marian was inside with her sewing machine. She made her own prom dress her junior and senior year in high school. The styles were classy and fashionable. When it came to boys, she and Alexandra had a sisterly rival going on. Marian and Bonnie also had their share of sisterly rivalry, though, not over boys. It was the everyday sister envy stuff. Marian was the defender and protector of her own point of view. She didn't shrink from threat, challenge, difficulty or rivalry.

Bonnie, the humble and spiritual one of the family, the middle child. Care free and relaxed in nature, Bonnie sometimes goes about life at an easy going pace convenient for her. Henry Sr. called her, "*The problem child*," because when life did not go as she expected it to go; she felt no one understood her. She would go off walking by herself. Sometimes the family would have to form a search party to look for her.

Most often, she was found in the back of the family's home, sitting under the tree. She would tell Henry Sr. and Katie to just leave her alone and let her sit there and think. Thinking problems through and examining them from all sides were important to her. She had a way of looking at the world that made perfect sense sometimes only to her. Bonnie did enjoy going roller skating with Jocelyn and Henry Jr. She also found delight in going to church. When she was not off to herself, reading or skating; she was attending church services at Revelations Baptist Church on Jefferson Avenue. She could not sing a lick, but she was a member of the choir.

Spoiled described Henry Jr... He insisted on having the world move in his direction and at his speed. His way or no way is a short statement befitting Henry Jr.'s character. He often reacted negatively to those trying to stand between him and any toy or game he wanted. Stubborn, yet willing to take a risk, made him unique in his own right. His advantage, he was the only boy in the family and everyone, sort of, let him get his way.

Jocelyn and Henry are only a year apart and they fought all the time. They fought hard, but loved each other much. Henry Jr. always wanted his way. If Jocelyn wanted vanilla ice cream, Henry Jr. would want chocolate and on and on. To keep both children happy, Katie bought both kinds.

Despite his daring personality, he loved his family. The connection with his father illustrated a sense of realness. He loved and admired Henry Sr. Henry Jr. would spend hours with his father. They worked to repair televisions in the house. They played pool on the pool table in the basement of the home. They played card games and watched football together. Wherever Henry Sr. went, Henry Jr. wanted to go with him. Henry Sr. wanted to set a good example for his son.

At around nine years old, Henry Sr. sat Henry Jr. in the car and taught him the basics of how to drive. During travel, Henry Sr. instructed Henry Jr. on how to read a map. Henry Jr. sat right up front between his father and mother and helped navigate the way to their destination. By the time Henry Jr. was ten, he could tell you exactly how to get from Buffalo to Martinsville. He knew all the toll roads and rest stops along the way. Katie loved that Henry Jr. was the sidekick, giving her the ability to sleep along the way.

Henry Sr. had a special relationship with all five of his children. He spent the most time with Henry Jr. and Jocelyn. They were the youngest. Henry Sr., well into his sixties, had slowed down some. He had a terrible cough that kept him awake many nights. He sometimes slept sitting up on the couch. Jocelyn always saw him sitting on the couch with his head hung low. His head often dropped into his hands like a storm-broken flower. When he started coughing, Jocelyn ran to get him a glass of water. She thought maybe it was the Camel cigarettes he smoked. She had no idea that he had black lung disease. He developed the condition from working in the coal mines, inhaling coal dust over a long period. The effects caused severe chest pains and shortness of breath.

There is no current or past cure for black lung disease. Seeing the distressed look on her father's face disturbed Jocelyn. It was tough to see her father when he got into his coughing spells. He would insist that he was okay. He never let the disease stop him from spending time with his family. He continued his work as a brick mason.

Jocelyn had a special birthday the year she turned nine. Her father packed as many children from Cayuga Street in his Lincoln Mark IV and took them all downtown to the movie theater. They went to see the Walt Disney movie *Herbie the Love Bug Goes to Monte Carlo*. It was a story about Herbie, an animated talking, white Volkswagen beetle racing car, with a mind of its own. Jocelyn picked the movie and Henry Sr. made sure she enjoyed her ninth birthday with friends.

Katie had her children involved in different activities to keep them busy. Bonnie, Henry Jr. and Jocelyn's favorite past time was going skating at *Skateland* on E. Ferry Street. Katie, Katrina's grandparents and Deanna's mother from Cayuga Street would all take turns taking the children to the skating rink. Buffalo's winters were tough, but the snow never stopped the group from going skating.

One winter, an unexpected snow storm hit while the group was at the skating rink. The snow had fallen rapidly and halted all travel, cars buried in snow. Katie had no way to get the group home from the skating rink. Jocelyn, Bonnie, Henry Jr., Sheena and Katrina had to walk from West Ferry to Cayuga street in the storm. The walk home was long and the temperature was near freezing. However, they made it home safely. Their hands and feet were frost bitten. The snow cleared by the next weekend. The group was back at *Skateland*.

Bonnie, Henry Jr., Sheena and Katrina were also a part of the Priderette's drill team and marching band. Mr. Adams founded the drill team. Mrs. Adams was responsible for the girls on the step team. Mr. Adams was responsible for the boys in the marching band. Rigorous practices kept the members of the team busy. The drill team competed in local and state competitions as well as participated in the Juneteenth parade each year. The parents were proud of the children and their achievements.

Sheena and Katrina lived with their great-grandparents, however, their grandmother, Ms. Hanson, lived next door to Sheena and Katrina. Ms. Hanson would let Sheena, Katrina, Bonnie, Henry Jr., Deanna and Jocelyn hang out at her home. The group watched movies on the cable channels. The first time Jocelyn saw the movie *Mahogany*, starring Diana Ross and Billy Dee Williams was at Ms. Hanson's house. She saw the movie *Car Wash* starring Richard Pryor and Otis Day as well. Ms. Hanson popped popcorn for the group and made Kool-Aid for them to drink. Jocelyn enjoyed many fun times with friends and family from Cayuga Street.

ALBERTA LAMPKINS

Eight

Time to See the World!

The freedom of travel kindled enthusiasm and interest for the Harris family. Henry and Katie often loaded all five children in Henry's metallic blue Lincoln Mark IV. The family packed sandwiches for the road and drove across highways and byways. They ventured into Martinsville and other places at least twice a year. The memorable moments filled Jocelyn with joy. The family traveled through mountains and passed by historical landmarks.

Henry made a point of stopping at notable places. Places such as Walton's Mountain in Schuyler, Virginia, the actual place that inspired the television series *Walton's Mountain*. Henry wanted his family to have the chance and opportunity to see parts of the world through travel.

The atmosphere in Martinsville was radically different from upstate New York. The people talked differently, dressed differently and acted differently. They said "Yes, ma'am" and "No, ma'am" a lot. Charmed by their southern accents, Jocelyn had a fit of laughter hearing the locals speak. She thought it funny to hear Henry Sr. talk at times. "Go on up yonder." Henry Sr. couldn't escape his southern roots.

The steep hills frequently caused a grip of attention. Jocelyn's eyes would widen going down the hills. She often clenched her mother's arm with one hand and her stomach with the other hand. The funny feeling made her feel weightless. Henry drove up and down the hills like a pro without a flinch; he was clearly familiar with the roads in Martinsville.

The story of Katie eating dirt the hue of red brought a flash of humor to the family. Jocelyn wondered if Katie ever had the urge to have another taste. Fluttering laughter filled her mind at the thought.

"It tastes good to me," Katie explained without shame.

Boundless admiration consumed Jocelyn. Traveling with her parents and being in the place where they grew as children into adulthood was meaningful to Jocelyn.

A trace of bitterness found its way into Jocelyn's heart.   The opportunity to meet both sets of grandparents ended before her arrival. She had a hazy recollection of her great-grandfather George.   Katie and her sister Jocelyn brought their grandfather from Martinsville to live in Buffalo.   George lived in the home with Jocelyn.   Katie and Jocelyn took turns caring for their ailing grandfather. He stayed a short time before he passed away in Jocelyn's home.

The two sisters had his body transported to Martinsville.   He wanted to be buried in his hometown. He was laid to rest next to his beloved wife. The Harris family plot stood tall in the Colored People's Cemetery down on Second Street.   George would be the last member of the family buried there. For a while Katie's aunt paid a grave digger to keep the plots cleaned up. She died in 1984. The graveyard is now unkempt and overgrown. No record of who is buried there exists. There are more than a hundred years of unrecorded plots in an unnamed graveyard. That is a travesty of itself.

The smell of moth balls and chitterlings waved through Jocelyn's nose upon entering the home of Ms. Hastings. Jocelyn disliked the odor. The torn screen door remained the same each year and each visit. The furniture in the home was mismatched. A couch, different types and style chairs filled the home. Sheets covered cushions on the couch to mask its well-worn age. Pictures of family and friends scattered about the home. Jocelyn felt an apprehensive dread entering the home. Ms. Hastings' exhilarating charm was infectious. Ms. Hastings knew Katie and Henry Sr. well and she welcomed the Harris family anytime they were in town. Fried chicken, macaroni and cheese, cornbread, chitterlings, collard greens and ham cooked up and waiting for the family. Jocelyn absolutely refused to eat chitterlings. Quite frankly, she picked over the meal. She could not get over the smell of moth balls and chitterlings in the home. Ms. Hastings enjoyed the visit with the family and Katie and Henry

Sr. felt comfortable in her home. Jocelyn respected her parents' friendship with Ms. Hastings and never complained about visiting.

The folks in Martinsville still called Henry Sr. "Mr. Big Shot." Jocelyn felt like a little big shot when they arrived in town. The children around Jocelyn's age and her siblings' age, found the Harris family cultured. The mention of being from New York drew attention. Questions about what life was like in New York amused Jocelyn. A little star from Buffalo shared her stories. The crowd loved her embellished truths.

The family stayed one of two places when they were in town. The Henry Hotel formerly located on Broad and East Church Street or the Holiday Inn. Once the family settled in, Henry Sr. made his routine trip to the "Alley" off of Fayette and Barton Street. He laughed, joked and had a few drinks with friends. He brought the children by to say hello to his friends, but they stayed a short time. Henry never drank in front of his children. The respect Henry Sr. received in Martinsville shouted approval by Jocelyn. She treasured Henry's worthy achievements. She bubbled with pride.

Jocelyn understood through the family's travels to Virginia, Maryland, Washington D.C, Kentucky and Ohio, Henry's purpose. He wanted to give his family an opportunity to see the world through different lenses. Wanted them to not be afraid to explore and experience life. It was simply a fleeting moment in time. Jocelyn's love for Henry Sr. and her family smiled like an unclouded sun.

The trip to Jocelyn's aunt Lynette's house in Maryland was always pleasant. Lynette married the son of a prominent preacher and bore two children, Calvin and Carla. The family lived in a middle-class area in Maryland in a beautiful home with a well-manicured lawn. Lynette, a devout Christian, remained faithful to her religious practice. Never uttering a curse word or taking a drink of alcohol. Calvin and Carla made sure the cousins had a good time during visits. Memories of visiting the White House with Calvin and Carla stand out in Jocelyn's mind. Walking the halls where great

Presidents lived delighted Henry Jr. and Jocelyn. Jocelyn loved her aunt Lynette and cousins, but the distance kept them from being close. The relationship with her namesake differed.

ALBERTA LAMPKINS

Nine

For goodness namesake.

iss Lady, that's the name Jocelyn's aunt kindly called her. It tickled her heart every time she heard the words. The sound of her aunt's voice was calm like a flowing river and Jocelyn admired her aunt's vanity and womanlike loveliness. The way she treated Jocelyn and her siblings took root in their hearts.

Aunt Jocelyn didn't have any children of her own. She'd wanted children, prayed for children, but never had one. Jocelyn wondered why God gave some people children and others not. Her aunt was *Mommy* material from her point of view. Who has the authority to interrogate God? No one, Jocelyn guessed.

The love Aunt Jocelyn would have given to her own children poured onto her sister's. The devoted attachment to those she did not birth showed the

79

beauty of her character. The bonds were, in a way, the same, yet different with each of her sister's children. Alexandra, the oldest niece spent the most time with her. The others felt no void. She made them all feel loved.

When Aunt Jocelyn sensed rivalry between Alexandra and Marian, or Marian and Bonnie, she gave them all a talk. She would prance over to the house then line all three girls on the couch next to each other. Aunt Jocelyn would put her hands on her hips and proceed to point out the causes and circumstances of their behavior. All three girls sat hushed. Their eyes stood open in speechless surprise.

"Now listen. This unnecessary bickering needs to stop! You are sisters. Sisters should love each other. Sisters care and support each other. I want you to apologize to each other and I don't want to hear about you not getting along again. Now, don't let me have to come back over here for this! You are not going to worry my sister to death!"

Aunt Jocelyn left them feeling misty and propelled to forgive each other.

The title *namesake* had a profound meaning for Jocelyn. She looked forward to spending time with her aunt. Sometimes all five children stayed the night. Other times each had his or her own evening. Jocelyn treasured her single moments with her aunt. They shared a meal, watched a movie and simply talked. When the hour of darkness fell, Jocelyn often sat on the edge of her aunt's bed. She watched her put pink rollers in her hair that hung down long. Then she put cold cream on her face and did the same for Jocelyn. They talked about everything. Much of the talk expressed instructions about life.

Peace and stillness wrapped around Jocelyn's soul when she was with her aunt. The morning would come and her aunt would put a kettle of water on the stove for tea. The two sipped tea and talked more.

"Miss Lady. It is important you remember to always, be a lady. You have a sweet spirit. I want you to keep that. I want you to stay just as you are. Now, there are going to be difficult things that happen in life. And you may not always understand the reasons. But, I want you to remember this. In difficult moments, just lift your head up to God and say, "Lord, teach me how to fly. God will help you soar above any problem. He will show you how to make it through the difficult times. You just have to be willing to listen to him and be willing to learn. A good child of God is always willing to learn! One day, you will remember this and you will understand. God teaches his most precious people how to fly and how to be free to enjoy his love and enjoy life."

Aunt Jocelyn shared a powerful message with her namesake. A message that Jocelyn has never forgot. Whenever Uncle Franklin entered the kitchen and asked what the two were talking about, aunt Jocelyn would say, "Girl Talk." There was nothing more for Uncle Franklin to say after that.

Jocelyn got along well with her uncle. His striking character and love for her aunt made him a good person to Jocelyn. Being twenty years older than her aunt gave him the air of wise counsel. Providing a home and caring for his wife sat high on his list of priorities. Tall in height and lean in stature added influence to his persona. Certain Native American tribes had close relations with African Americans and Franklin was the product of this mixed race. His wavy hair needed only a gentle brush or smoothed with his hand. Shades of gray mixed with black glistened with sparkling splendor. Uncle Franklin kept a picture of his Native American mother on his dresser. Her cordial smile in the picture gave her a refined look. Franklin adored her picture like it was his most valuable possession. He often held the picture in his hands and stared. A tear trickled down his face whenever he thought of her. It was obvious; he cared deeply for his beloved mother.

The gift of gab came easy for Franklin. He shared creative and inventive stories. His listeners often had to use a searchlight for truth among his jumbled facts. The stories were amusing and clever in nature.

"You know, I once played in the band with Duke Ellington. I played the horn, and I played mighty good, I must add. I was just a young musician, but boy oh boy did I learn a lot from them cats. I remember one time….." Franklin would chuckle and go on for about an hour with his story.

Franklin once stated that he traveled horse back with the "Old Calvary" and drove the getaway car for Al Capone. Al Capone, one of the world's most notorious gangsters selected Franklin to be his chauffer. He told his stories with such elegance and grace, Jocelyn believed him. Not so much for Henry. Jocelyn's father didn't buy into Franklin's exaggerated and imaginative stories like Jocelyn.

"Franklin, you know you never drove a getaway car for Al Capone!"

Henry called to question Franklin's ripe reflections. The shade of doubt caused Franklin to burst into confidence.

"Man, you don't know what you talking about. I did too drive for Al Capone! I remember the last time I drove….."

Franklin continued on like an endless river. Henry Sr. found enjoyment poking holes in Franklin's stories. Definite and memorable moments of the two brothers-in-law sitting on the porch immersed in debate.   Jocelyn would burst into laughter listening to the two men converse.   She defined it as *friendly chatter* among family.

The people and families on Peach Street roused Jocelyn's interest.   The street felt alive and full of action. One did not have to watch television; entertainment stood outside their doors. Franklin and Jocelyn's aunt were good neighbors to their Peach Street family. They knew most all the families on the street. Well, they knew the neighbors between Peach Street and Carlton Street and the Kensington Expressway.   Franklin often gave the children candy and gum when they were playing outside or in front of the house.   Whenever Jocelyn visited, she sat outside with Uncle Franklin and watched the children at play. One particular day stood out.

"Tasha."   Uncle Franklin called one of Mrs. Barker's kids to the porch. "This is my niece Jocelyn. Would you like to play with her?"

"Sure," Tasha responded.

"You want to play kick the can with us?" Tasha welcomed her new friend.

85

"Okay, yes. I want to play." Jocelyn felt it was okay to be friends with Tasha.

Tasha played kick the can with her younger sister and the boy next door to her, Lamar. Tasha, Tasha's sister, Lamar and Jocelyn became instant friends. Jocelyn liked Tasha's personality. A bit of spiciness and natural wit defined her character. Tasha's ability to find humor in the most interesting situations amazed Jocelyn. Every day from then on was an adventure being friends with Tasha. She imitated the people on the street in a joyful way and brought everyone within the sound of her voice cheer. From the moment Jocelyn and Tasha met, their friendship became authenticated.

Mrs. Barker, Tasha's mother, set the ground rules and her children complied. If they didn't, well, she knew how to keep them in line. Mrs. Barker believed that it takes a community to raise a child. And she had some degree of influence on the other children of Peach Street. All the young people knew that Mrs. Barker had a watchful eye and looked out for their best interest.

It's not that there is anything fancy about Peach Street, but being on the street gave Jocelyn a sense of indescribable reverence. It was a homelike and lively atmosphere on the street. On any given summer day or night the folks on Peach Street could be found outside. Sitting on their porches to catch a breeze and giving an ear to a little neighborly gossip.

Johnny lived across the street from the Barkers. He drank way too much. On any given day he had a bottle of Wild Irish Rose or Thunderbird drink in hand. His girlfriend drank equally as much. The two fussed, cussed and argued with each other all day and night. They would make up and start the same show over the next day.

Holding his pants up with one hand and his liquor in the other hand, Johnny often stumbled to the street.

"All ya'll M-F's can kiss my @!!" Quibbling and stuttering his speech. Swaying back and forth and fighting to keep his balance. Without failure, he staggered up the street to the corner store. He always had to have a bottle in hand and one in his pocket. It was downright nonsense, yet entertainment also.

"Go sit your old dusty self-down, Johnny! "These kids don't need to hear all that mess you talkin."

Mrs. Barker put Johnny in his place. Johnny would cuss everybody out, but not Mrs. Barker.

When Johnny sobered up, he helped his neighbors. He often ran errands to the store, shoveled snow, cut grass and any other tedious duty to help his neighbors. He had a good heart, but just had a hard life. Mrs. Barker knew this. She fixed plates of food for him and made sure he ate.

Ms. Brewer lived between the Barkers and Jocelyn's aunt and uncle. Her grandchildren visited weekly, however she never allowed them outside to play with the other children on Peach Street. She went to church on Sunday morning and did her weekly grocery shopping Sunday evening. The rest of the days she spent locked up in her house. She peered out her window from time to time. If anyone so much as stood in front of her house, she yelled at them to move along. Sometimes the young folks stood in front of her house on purpose, just to hear her fuss. It gave Jocelyn and Tasha a reason to laugh. They may have mumbled a few mean things about Ms. Brewer under their breath, but they always remained respectful.

Jackie, one of Tasha's older sisters, had graduated from cosmetology school. She opened a beauty shop on the corner of Peach and Carlton Street. Jocelyn and Tasha earned a few dollars sweeping up between customers. The soft colors painted on the wall relaxed the customers. Women and men received trims, cuts, curls, straightening, perms, highlights, shampooing, conditioning, hair extensions and a multitude of other services at the shop. Outside of hair, the shop was alive and full of current gossip. Jocelyn and Tasha pretended not to listen. However, their young ears laid glued to the blissful conversations.

Humor came easy for Jackie as it did for Tasha. Her contagious wit and crisp dialogue brought elevated enjoyment to the shop. Her skillful way of joking with her patrons and visitors inspired hilarious outburst of laughter every day.

"Girl, what inspired you to walk out the house with that outfit on?"

"You know that checkered shirt don't match them bell bottom pants!"

"Old Jacob must have said you look good. And you know he blind in one eye and can't see out the other!" A roar of laughter filled the air.

To the outside, the Fruit belt was just an urban ghetto, but to Jocelyn, it was a place filled with delightful spiciness. Jocelyn felt a sense of freedom when she hung out with Tasha. She could be herself and never have to apologize for not being perfect. Jocelyn and Tasha declared a sisterhood. Their pioneering spirit led them through the good, the bad and the unexpected. Like the one lazy summer afternoon when the girls walked around the Fruit belt. They stopped to watch Lamar and some of the other guys in the neighborhood play flag football. They cheered and encouraged the game along. Watching the game was fine. However, after the friendly game of flag football, the mood changed.

Jocelyn and Tasha joked and horsed around with their friend Lamar and his friend Branson. Call it puppy love, but distinct feelings of attraction developed. In the midst of their childhood play, the four youngsters decided to test out kissing. Tasha kissed Branson. It was her first kiss. Jocelyn kissed Lamar. It was her first kiss. The kiss was soft and sweet and innocent. As quick as it started, the kiss was promptly interrupted. The four failed to scan the area for onlookers. There appeared Tasha's younger sister Trina.

"Ooh, I am going to tell Momma!" Trina taunted her sister.

"Soooo. If you tell, I'm going to tell Momma what you did yesterday!"

"You need to go find your own friends and leave us alone!" Tasha's words sparked a bit of fury in Trina.

"She is not going to tell. Forget Trina." Tasha brushed off the threat of imminent danger.

Instead of leaving the scene, the four stayed put. And before they knew it, Mrs. Barker showed up with a switch in hand.

"What you think y'all doing round here?"

"And you, Miss Lady, I'm going to tell your aunt. And you, Lamar, I'm going to tell your grandmother." She only had a few words for Branson. "Get your bug-eyed self out of here!" It was kind of funny, but not to the girls, at least, not at that moment.

"All y'all get your tails out of here." Mrs. Barker was not happy.

"Momma, we didn't do ......"

Before Tasha could get another word out her mouth, Mrs. Barker went to swatting that switch. Tasha tried to run, but she wasn't fast enough. Mrs. Barker laid into to Tasha all the way home. Lamar's friend Branson took off away from the scene. Jocelyn and Lamar stood in fear. Jocelyn felt bad for her friend and for herself. As promised, Mrs. Barker told Jocelyn's aunt and Lamar's grandmother.

With hands on her hips and a stern look on her face, Jocelyn's aunt shook her head.

"Now, now, now Miss Lady. This is not how a young lady behaves!"

She sat Jocelyn down. She talked to her about boys and girls and why kissing was not a good idea. Jocelyn's heart sank at the thought of disappointing her aunt.

"Lamar is a good kid, but you two are way too young to be pretending to be grown and kissing."

Aunt Jocelyn went on for at least forty-five minutes talking to Jocelyn and counseling her on the ways of life. Aunt Jocelyn didn't yell, didn't strike Jocelyn, she just gave her wise words.

On the other side, after Mrs. Barker finished with Tasha, she was punished and confined to the porch for the rest of the day. Tasha sat looking sad. That is until Jocelyn sneaked over to sit with her. Lamar heard Jocelyn and Tasha talking from inside his grandmother's house. He peered out the window to make sure Mrs. Barker was nowhere in sight and then came out from his grandmother's house.

"Tasha, are you okay?" Lamar whispered with concern.

"Yes, I'm okay. Momma tore my butt up!" Tasha busted out in laughter. It was hilarious once they all thought about it. Only Tasha could find humor in the strangest of situations. Tasha imitated how her mother came around the corner to find them. And all three laughed until their stomachs hurt.

Mrs. Barker never once interfered with Jocelyn and Tasha's friendship. She allowed Jocelyn to still come around, spend the night and hang out with their family. She probably knew that the girls were just experiencing life.

Jocelyn and Lamar never talked about that kiss again. It was a sweet kiss. The kiss never led to anything further. Jocelyn, Lamar and Tasha remained friends. Jocelyn and Tasha would go on to have many childhood experiences together. They found other ways to entertain their young hearts.

The Neighborhood House Association located on Orange Street served as the recreational center for all the young people in the Fruit Belt. The center offered many activities, such as arts and crafts, dance, basketball, games, summer camps, and many other activities. Jocelyn later, along with Tasha became a member of the Neighborhood House Drill Team, led by Beverly Nathan. This activity kept them busy. They practiced all the time. Ms. Nathan, which everyone loving called Beverly, was like a big sister or a great aunt to them all. She made sure everyone's uniform and boots were squared away. She genuinely cared about the young people in the neighborhood and treated everyone like her family.

The drill and step team competed in local competitions. The team performed in the Drill O Rama held each year at the convention center in downtown Buffalo. The Drill O Rama was an avenue for drill and step teams across Buffalo to display their talents and creativity. It was high energy with fancy steppers and Jocelyn loved the thrill of being a part of the team. The Neighborhood House Drill Team also participated in the annual Juneteenth Festival, an exploration and celebration of the last remaining slaves in the United States. Jefferson Street would be blocked off and there would be parades, park parties, cookouts and street fairs. It was full of excitement and an important event for African Americans and others who came out for the festivities.

Ten

Fire before the storm.

There are some moments in life that catch you by surprise. An electrical fire started in the attic of Jocelyn's family home on Cayuga Street. The fire spread throughout the roof and caused severe destruction to the home. Luckily, no one was hurt. The family got out before the fire intensified. The fire spread quickly and damaged a lot in the inside of the home. The brick exterior remained intact, however the furniture, clothing and appliances ruined.

The Red Cross put the family up in a hotel for three nights and gave them a voucher from *Twin Fair*, a local department store located on E. Ferry Street. The family shopped and replaced some items lost in the fire.

Anyway, Henry Sr. and his family moved in with Aunt Jocelyn and Uncle Franklin. Henry Sr. spent a lot of his days at the home on Cayuga with his brothers working to restore and repair the home. His goal was for his family to return to their own home. He worked day and night. Henry Jr. and Jocelyn continued to attend school thirty-nine and walked to school from their Aunt Jocelyn's house.

During recess, faithfully, Jocelyn ran over to the fence to see her father. She waved at him and her uncles. The brothers worked side by side, laying out wood and other materials to repair the home. Jocelyn's father was determined to make the home better than before. Jocelyn was proud of the work her father did and anxious to see how the house would look when he finished.

Henry Sr. would come to Aunt Jocelyn and Franklin's house exhausted. His breathing and shortness of breath increased. It got so bad that Katie took Henry Sr. to see his doctor at the Veteran's hospital, on Bailey Avenue. He was kept at the hospital for observation and stayed for over a week. The whole family visited him every day. For Katie and all five children to see him at the same time, Henry Sr. came down to the lobby in his hospital robe and pants and sat with them. He would laugh and play around with the family. He also talked about what new things he planned to do to the house when he got out of the hospital. Henry Sr. made plans for the family to take a trip to Martinsville for the following Easter. Before leaving Henry at the hospital each night, he had a message for his family.

"No matter what happens, you are family and I want you to always, stick together!"

Jocelyn never left the hospital before giving him a kiss on the forehead. "See you tomorrow, Daddy." Jocelyn smiled, anticipating visiting Henry Sr. the next day.

ALBERTA LAMPKINS

Eleven

No rainbow in the sky.

It was a cool day in September. The sun shined bright, but there was not much warmth radiating. Autumn leaves rustled about and took flight as a gentle, but unfriendly wind blew. Jocelyn and Henry Jr. walked to school from their Aunt Jocelyn's house as they had done for weeks. They both were unusually quiet and didn't have a fight on the way to school. The two arrived at school on time and each went to their classrooms. It was a normal school day until Jocelyn and Henry Jr. were summoned to the principal's office. Their teachers informed them to gather all their belongings and take them with them.

"Ooh, somebody in trouble with Dr. Dixon," their classmates snickered and laughed. They knew a walk to the principal's office was like the walk of death.

Jocelyn couldn't imagine why she was called to the office. Henry Jr. was the one who always got in trouble. She entered the office and saw Henry Jr. sitting in a chair. They both looked at each other like what is going on.

Dr. Dixon greeted Jocelyn and Henry Jr. and escorted them to his office. He sat them down in front of his desk.

"Your mother called and she needs the two of you to leave school. You have to go directly to your Aunt Jocelyn's house."

"Why?" both Jocelyn and Henry Jr. asked simultaneously.

"Your mother is waiting for you there. You will not be returning to school today. Your mother will explain everything when you get to your aunt's house."

Dr. Dixon walked the two to the doors exiting the school. He held the door open and watched them for as long as he could. Jocelyn and Henry Jr. didn't even try to guess what was wrong. They traveled silently.

The walk from High Street to Peach Street took forever, so it seemed for Jocelyn and Henry Jr. No one prepared them for the news they received when they arrived. Their Aunt Jocelyn waited for them on the porch. Once they approached the stairs to the porch, she hugged both of them and rushed them in the house. Alexandra, Marian and Bonnie were all there as well, all crying. Katie had a face full of tears and asked them to sit down.

"Your daddy passed away this morning at the hospital. He had a heart attack and the doctors could not revive him."

Henry Jr. started crying, kicking and screaming. Jocelyn didn't say a word. Bonnie left out of the house and went off walking. Marian went upstairs to be alone. Alexandra grabbed hold of Jocelyn.

"Jocelyn, did you hear what Mommy said? Daddy is gone, Jocelyn, Daddy is gone!"

Jocelyn just stood there. It was as if Jocelyn was having a bad dream and she was trying to wake up. Katie came to comfort Jocelyn, but Jocelyn was motionless. With assurance, Jocelyn announced, "My daddy is not gone anywhere. He is at the VA Hospital and I want to go see him now!"

A time of disillusion followed her words. It was a confused and troublesome moment.

Alexandra couldn't handle the situation. She left and went upstairs with Marian.

It wasn't until the day of the viewing of Henry Sr.'s body that Jocelyn finally shed tears. The viewing service was held at Thomas T. Edwards Funeral home on the corner of Strauss and Genesee Street. Jocelyn saw Henry Sr.'s body laid out in the casket. He laid there like a warrior taking his rest, his hands folded across his chest and she touched him. He felt cold. It finally hit her, her father was gone. Buckets of tears fell from her eyes and she held her hand over her daddy's hand.

"Daddy, Daddy, why did you leave me?" she whispered to him as if he could hear her. Time stood still, but the world kept spinning. She wanted him to hear her voice and wake up, but Henry Sr. laid there at rest. Jocelyn's body went limp and family members rushed to catch her. The room moved in slow motion for Jocelyn. When she looked up, she saw her friend Tasha, crying as hard as she was. Tasha ran to her side and held her hand.

"It's going to be okay, Jocelyn. Everything is going to be okay." Tasha felt Jocelyn's pain as only a true friend would.

A stretch black limousine pulled up to drive the family to the funeral and then to Forest Lawn Cemetery to bury Henry Sr. Cars lined up with flags affixed to the window and followed behind the family to the gravesite. Henry Sr. was buried with full military honors as a veteran of war. The honorary military played "Taps". The American flag draped Henry's casket. When the honors were complete, two service men dressed in Army uniforms wearing white gloves folded the American flag and handed it to Katie.

The casket lowered to the ground. Cries echoed in the cemetery when Henry Jr. screamed out.

"No, Daddy, no, Daddy, don't go. Take me with you, Daddy!"

Suddenly with one frog like movement, Henry Jr. tried to jump on the casket. He was restrained to prevent him from stopping the casket moving in the ground. Everyone in attendance saw the painful sight. The loss of Henry Sr. touched the entire family. Jocelyn felt a mixture of anger and disbelief. Jocelyn felt he left her too soon.

Henry Sr.'s dream to rebuild the family's home on Cayuga Street quickly shattered when he departed. His brothers tried their best to continue the work, but the weather got colder and the funds to rebuild depleted. The house stood empty for a long time until the bulldozers wiped it away. Jocelyn felt let down.

Katie had a hard time managing financial matters for the family. Henry Sr. had always taken care of the bills. Katie spent her money on her children and as she pleased. She was now the head of the household. And bills had to be paid. The family could not stay with her sister Jocelyn forever. Katie found a home on the upper east side of Buffalo to rent. Life for Jocelyn was never the same. She moved away from her friends on Cayuga Street and from her best friend Tasha on Peach Street.

Katie went from nursing at the hospital to working with elderly patients in their home. The schedule was more flexible and she could spend more time with the family. She received widow's pension and black lung benefits Henry Sr.'s death. Jocelyn didn't like being moved around, she wanted her house back. She wanted the house her father built for the family. The house that once stood upright on Cayuga Street.

Jocelyn's aunt invited her to visit and spend the night any time she wanted. Jocelyn took her up on the offer. Aunt Jocelyn felt compelled to be there for the family even more than she already had been. She was a God send to the family. Jocelyn's uncle Franklin was also very supportive. Hearing him tell his stories comforted Jocelyn. Jocelyn smiled and remembered how her father and her uncle would debate over the validity of Franklin's stories. It brought a bit of peace.

Aunt Jocelyn's house became Jocelyn's home away from home. Jocelyn cherished the relationship she had with her aunt and appreciated everything she did for the family. Jocelyn's aunt always consoled her when she was feeling down about losing her father. She would buy Jocelyn cards with good messages on them and she always signed the cards with *Love always, your namesake.*

Twelve

What a story!

Life seemed to have drifted out the chimney for Jocelyn. She wanted desperately to still feel connected to her father. A visit with Henry Sr.'s youngest sister, Aunt Mae helped. Aunt Mae's dazzling traits matched her shapely plump self and cheerful personality. The lightest shade of brown there could be, she looked almost cream in color. Her smooth skin and velvet brown eyes made her pleasantly attractive. Mae's silky long black wavy hair added to her vibrancy.

Jocelyn always felt comfortable with her Aunt Mae. She liked going to Mae's home. Her modern fancy furniture and elegant china displayed in a European style dining hutch stood out. The home represented Mae's taste for quality and her love for the finer things in life. A bundle of luxurious church hats in hat boxes filled one room in her home. And she had one of a kind dresses and suits to match each hat. The hats, church suits and shoes that could not find a home in her room, found a place in the living room. I don't think anyone dared to tell Mae she had too many clothes or too many church hats. Jocelyn chuckled at the thought of Mae nominated for the Sunday's Best Dressed list at her church. She never missed a Sunday service and never missed the opportunity to show off her hats. She deserved the title.

Mae's rich fashion sense coupled with her down to earth personality made her unequaled. The visit had a profound effect on Jocelyn. It was necessary for Jocelyn. Jocelyn knew Mae loved her brother as much as she loved her father. She wanted to know more of what Henry was like as a young man. That knowledge rested in Mae's heart. Mae gladly shared as many stories about Henry Sr. as she could. Mae knew that it didn't matter what story she shared with Jocelyn, it would all be meaningful.

A sympathetic gaze greeted Jocelyn as she entered Mae's home. She fought back the tears. Mae grabbed Jocelyn and gave her a hug. She offered her something to eat. It was usual of Mae to offer a meal. Mae kept plenty of food and snacks around, but Jocelyn was not hungry. She just needed a friendly family moment. Mae said all the things Jocelyn hoped to hear

"Your dad was something special. He was the rock of our family. He always looked out for me and all his brothers and sister. He also loved you and your siblings very much."

Jocelyn's heart filled as tears glistened down her cheeks.

It was cheerful chatter and Jocelyn became even more intrigued when Mae shared a story.

"Let me give you a narrative about someone you never met." She began telling Jocelyn this story:

"Picture this:

It was a cold winter's day in West Virginia. The year was February 1890. Men put extra logs in the fireplace and families huddled together under warm blankets. The wind whipped through the town, however, it ceased just before dawn on this particular day. Fluffy flakes of snow caressed

the Mountain tops and flurries fell humbly to the ground. Most of the people in town were safe and cuddled inside their homes. Oh, but for one woman, distress brewed in this quaint little country community. Remotely located on the far edge of the town, a poor man's gravesite stood alone. A slight chill made the abandoned field with grey stones scattered about feel eerie. The sun set and disappeared into the night. A lonely, grayish-brown barred owl with dark eyes and a small hooked bill stood perched in a tree. His squeal almost sounded human.

Oddly, a strange woman dressed in a dark blue hand-me-down dress appeared. Her tattered wool shawl draped around her, hid her plump, Hershey brown body as she approached the deserted field. She wore a pair of bruised and battered brown boots that reached just above her ankles. The footgear hardly kept her feet warm as she made small footsteps in the snow. She carried what seemed to be a sack of potatoes cradled in her hands. This made her presence in the snow covered field even more obscure.

Careful not to be noticed, she glanced around the field. When she saw no onlookers, she gently kneeled down. She began to weep in silence. Tears tried to fall down her face, but froze still. Slowly, she turned her head from side to side. She made a mental note of the placement of each grey stone that surrounded her. She pulled the sack in her hands close to her bosom. A gentle kiss landed on the top of the bundle. With precision and ease, she laid the sack down on the snow covered ground. The bundle lay beside an unmarked grave. She sat still for a moment, and then stood up. She didn't want to do it, but she had no other choice. She left the newborn baby girl wrapped in a blanket covered with burlap. The baby was just one day old. The woman left the baby girl unaccompanied as she discreetly departed from the field.

"Lawd, Lawd, please Lawd, forgive me," she whispered.

Jocelyn, half-delirious with bright alertness in her eyes, was confused. "Who is the lady? Why did she leave the baby?" Jocelyn anxiously waited to hear Mae's reply.

Mae told her that the baby was her grandmother and the lady that left her was a servant. "Your great-grandmother was Caucasian. She had a relationship with a black man that worked on the tobacco farm owned by her father. The Caucasian woman was a married woman. Her husband believed that the child she carried was his child."

Jocelyn had a startled look on her face, but wanted to hear the remaining story. Mae carried on.

"When it came time to birth the child, the Caucasian woman went away with her mid-wife, a black servant. When the baby was born and had features of a mulatto child, the woman panicked and told the servant to get rid of the child. She told the servant that she would tell her husband the child was stillborn. She would add that she buried the child because it was too painful to bring the stillborn child home."

"What happened next?" Jocelyn asked.

"The servant did as she told her to. She had a change of heart though and went back and got the baby. She took the baby to her black father and he took her in and cared for her."

"Wow," said Jocelyn.

"Your great-grandfather took a black wife to help him care for your grandmother. The beauty of your grandmother threatened the sanctity of her relationship with her. She was envious and mistreated your grandmother. Your grandmother was like a modern day Cinderella in that home." Mae cleared her throat and said with pride.

"When your grandmother turned sixteen years old, she saved up money she earned from the sale of clove oil. Back then, clove oil was used to make beauty products. She made enough money to catch a train and went as far as she could by railcar. She ended up in Bluefield, West Virginia and worked in a boarding house cooking and cleaning. That is where she met your grandfather, my daddy. My daddy, your grandfather was a dark colored man." Mae chuckled "My mother said she wanted a dark man for her children to have a darker shade than she did. Her mixed heritage caused her pain."

The astonishment of the story captivated Jocelyn. She had never heard this story. She had never really heard any stories of her grandparents. Mae grabbed a few framed pictures that had stood on end tables and the mantle of the fireplace.

"Here is a picture of your grandmother. And here is a picture of your grandfather. And here is a picture of your great-grandmother."

It was a picture of the Caucasian woman that left her child in an unmarked grave. She had been forgiven by her brown daughter.

Thirteen

Pain, pain, and go far, far away!

Two years had passed since Henry's death and a lot had changed. Jocelyn's heart still mourned his loss, but she found a glittering vision of delight with her family and friends. Her sister Marian married a young man from their current neighborhood and birthed the first grandchild of the family. He was cute and tiny and Jocelyn swallowed him up with love. When Marian's marriage failed, a sense of bitterness toward men pervaded her. Everyone pitched in to help care for her son, particularly Katie. Just as she did anything for her children, Katie did the same for her grandson.

Bonnie graduated from high school and attended Erie Community College. Henry Jr. graduated from the eighth grade and started school at Kensington High School. Jocelyn was in the eighth grade and continued at school thirty-nine. School thirty-nine's name changed to the Martin Luther King Multicultural Institute.

Alexandra went through a tough time in her life. She suffered from terrible migraine headaches and major health problems. The doctor prescribed pain medication to help ease the suffering. Along with the medication, she also continued smoking marijuana to try and disrupt the pain. The tablets prescribed altered her demeanor at times. The headaches and the symptoms of her health problems prevented her from working a steady job. Alexandra relied on help from Katie and from her Aunt Jocelyn. Katie did not like seeing Alexandra in pain and made sure she always had her medication available for her. Her experience in the nursing field and contacts with local doctors helped her get Alexandra the relief she needed. Alexandra became solely dependent on alleviating her discomfort with a pill. Things didn't get any better after the phone call from Jocelyn's uncle, Franklin. The hollow, cracked voice of Franklin on the phone sent a chill down Katie's spine, as she bellowed out a hollowing scream. Franklin broke the news that he woke up to find his beloved wife, Jocelyn resting in peace. She slipped away quietly in her sleep, never to open her eyes again.

Jocelyn couldn't believe the news. Her eyes limped with sadness. Tears, large and profuse flowed down her cheek. Katie gathered her five children and announced the parting of her dear sister, Jocelyn. Hysterical shrieks and resentful eyes from Katie, Alexandra, Marian, Bonnie, Henry Jr. and Jocelyn took over the space. It was a dreadful, unexpected day when they learned of the passing of their sister and aunt.

For years, Aunt Jocelyn suffered from Cancer and never told anyone. Jocelyn remembered when she stopped working, but Jocelyn's young age never caused her to question her aunt's unemployed status. Jocelyn grieved. She lost someone she admired, someone she loved. She lost her beloved namesake. Jocelyn had a frosty response to God. Angered, she questioned why she had to lose two of the most important people in her life. It was unfair and it was cruel, Jocelyn thought. Her whole being seethed as she became annoyed with feelings of loss.

Devastation rocked the residents of Peach Street. They learned that one of their own had gone on home to rest in heaven. One by one or two by two, neighbors brought food and desserts to Franklin's home. Jocelyn wanted to be there and there she was to welcome the mourners as they shared pleasant stories and memories of her delightful and loving aunt whom she thought the world of. Lamar and Tasha were there to support their friend.

Tasha started by saying, "Jocelyn, you remember when Ms. Jocelyn used to put her hands on her hips and say, 'Now, now, now Miss Lady, that's not how a young lady should act.'"

Jocelyn had a sudden bellow of laughter. Tasha did a near perfect imitation of her aunt and it was comforting. Jocelyn never took her friendship with Tasha for granted. Friendships are invaluable, Jocelyn learned. *"Always be a lady."* The sound of her aunt's warm, flattering voice flowed in Jocelyn's mind and soothed her spirit.

Alexandra took the death of Aunt Jocelyn hard. She was never the same again. She withdrew. Masked in her black lashes and pale blue eye shadow, unspoken words laid deep inside her eyes. Her heart dissolved to her toes and she felt abandoned and empty. Alexandra was prescribed a drug that was intended to help with depression, but crookedly caused a habit even harder to break. Katie understood something about Alexandra that no one else did. She protected Alexandra and reminded Marian, Bonnie, Henry Jr. and Jocelyn that they were a family and family always sticks together. Aunt Jocelyn would forever be missed.

ALBERTA LAMPKINS

Fourteen

Break dancing around my heart.

J ocelyn spent time sitting on Aunt Jocelyn and Uncle Franklin's porch. Aunt Jocelyn may have been gone, but not her memories. *Now, now, now Miss Lady.* Jocelyn could hear her aunt's voice in the wind.

Tasha sat with Jocelyn whenever she needed her to. The bond between Jocelyn and Tasha stood the test of time. They each had other friends, but that didn't matter. Their friendship was built on mutual respect and the freedom of knowing that nothing would ever come between them. They did almost everything together and lived without regrets. Summers always brought new experiences. And the summer of nineteen eighty-two proved that.

Jocelyn and Tasha planned to go roller skating around the Fruit Belt neighborhood. The two friends stopped to pick up their friend Doris. All three ladies headed off on skates to the Neighborhood House on Orange Street. Doris told Jocelyn and Tasha that Ralph, the "break dancing guy" and his cousins were spotted at the Neighborhood House playing basketball. They arrived on the scene. One of the guys hanging outside at the community center had his boom box blaring and challenged Ralph to a dance off.

The hint of summer in the air and Afrika Bambaata and Soulsonic Force's song *Planet Rock* echoing in the atmosphere hyped up the crowd. Ralph pushed his sleeves up, adjusted his pants and went to work. Ralph entranced the audience with his smooth moves and fancy footwork. Break dancing is an art form for the skilled. Ralph had the skills and pleased the crowd with his movements. The precision in which he moved captivated his audience. It was a sight to see. The crowd cheered with delight and others envied his acrobatic style and original moves.

While the teens were reveling over the break dancers, Tasha gave Ralph's cousin, Shawn, a long calculated look. Something about him and the popular

Jerri curl he sported caught Tasha's interest. Ralph won the dance off hands down and he and his cousins headed home. Tasha innocently convinced Jocelyn and Doris to accompany her in following Ralph, Shawn and Shawn's brother Morris to the boys' *McCarley Gardens* housing area. The girls let their hair stream wild as the wind, caused by their roller skates, smacked them in the face. They were laughing, joking and thrilled with girlish joy. Ralph, Shawn and Morris glanced back at them and the girls giggled even more.

When the young ladies reached the Mulberry Street Bike Bridge that crossed over to Michigan Ave, Jocelyn decided to show off her skating abilities. Underestimating her ability to stop, she streamed down the ramp of the bridge. Unfortunately, she lost control and crashed into the rails on the bridge. Jocelyn's ankle swelled up to the size of a grapefruit. The three boys along with Tasha and Doris rushed over to help Jocelyn. Unable to walk on her own, Ralph, Shawn and Morris helped carry her to her Uncle Franklin's house. Her uncle called her mother and Katie rushed home from work. Katie whisked her off to Erie Community Medical Center or commonly called, ECMC, where Jocelyn underwent extensive surgery. Her fractured ankle in two places caused her hospitalization for five days. Pins put in both sides of her ankle. She was obligated to wear a cast set from her foot to her knee, for the rest of that summer.

The distance from the Fruit belt and McCarley Gardens to ECMC was quite a long way. However, Ralph, Shawn, Morris, Tasha and Doris took the bus and visited Jocelyn in the hospital. Ralph brought Jocelyn flowers. She was impressed that he thought enough to bring her flowers. Jocelyn also appreciated that her friends came to see about her.

Jocelyn spent the rest of the summer at her uncle's house on Peach Street. It was easier for her that way since she was in a cast. Tasha, her faithful friend sat on the porch with her every day. The two played *Jacks* with a little bouncy ball and ten silver jacks to see how many they could pick up before the ball hit the ground. They played board games and card games and anything to keep them entertained while Jocelyn was incapacitated with her cast.

Ralph and Shawn also came by to check on Jocelyn and visit with Tasha. Budding relationships bloomed between Ralph and Jocelyn and Shawn and Tasha. Once the cast was off and High School started Ralph and Jocelyn, Shawn and Tasha became inseparable. Even with Jocelyn attending Grover Cleveland High School, Ralph attending McKinley High School and both Tasha and Shawn attending South Park High School. It was all fun, until Ralph broke Jocelyn's heart. His break dancing moves, best dressed status and popularity with the girls got the best of him. And to be honest, they were really too young for love anyway. Ralph and Jocelyn may not have worked out, but her friendship with Tasha never wavered.

Jocelyn could not rid the notion of missing her aunt, missing her father and her home on Cayuga Street. Peach Street became her solace. As soon as she entered the Fruit belt and made her way to the corner she saw that bent up sign directing her towards her uncle Franklin and Tasha's home and her concerns flew out her mind. The street named after an orchard tree represented peace, laughter, joy and stability for Jocelyn. No matter where Katie moved the family to, Jocelyn could always go back to her namesake's house. It would still be standing, unlike her home on Cayuga. She could count on Tasha always being there to share a laugh or a memorable moment. Uncle Franklin made her still feel linked to her aunt Jocelyn as well.

"You know your aunt Jocelyn came to visit me last night," Franklin said to Jocelyn. Jocelyn was pleasant and replied, "Oh yeah?" Franklin crossed his skinny long legs and chuckled. He sat back in his recliner.

"Yeah, she was fussing at me about staying up too late watching television. I told her, 'aw honey, I'll go to bed as soon as Perry Mason goes off.'"

A tear like silver glistened in the corner of his eye.

"It must have been pleasing to hear her voice," Jocelyn replied with kindred sympathies. Franklin gave Jocelyn a radiant smile.

Tears of defeat blinded her eyes and her heart sang a wistful note for her uncle. He really believed he saw his deceased wife.

"Your aunt is always with me."

Jocelyn's heart melted like an ice cream cone on a hot July day. She knew at that moment, her aunt and her father were always going to be in her heart as well.

Fifteen

Time stands still for no one.

K atie worked day and night caring for her elderly patients. She had become like a piece of lead with wings on it; she never did anything for herself and gave up trying to take flight. All that she did benefitted Alexandra, Marian, Bonnie, Henry Jr., Jocelyn and her grandson. There wasn't anything that she would not do for her children. Even if it meant giving up a life of her own. Katie never quite mastered one stable place after the death of Henry. She moved the family around and only stayed long enough to make a temporary mark. Jocelyn did not understand why Katie had a hard time setting up solid roots after the death of Henry.

Marian, Jocelyn's sister, remained employed full-time and took her job as a single mom seriously. After Marian had her second son and the relationship with his father became unbearable, she left Buffalo and moved to Maryland to live near Lynette, Katie's younger sister. Bonnie completed her Associates degree at Erie Community College, married and then joined the Air Force. She went on to have three children and eventually separated from her first husband. Later, Bonnie completed two Master's Degrees and a Doctorate Degree.

Henry Jr. started an apprenticeship in screen printing and worked in several states before returning to Buffalo. Alexandra graduated from beauty school; however, she met an older man who provided well for her. She continued to battle health problems and depression. Jocelyn went away to college at Fredonia State University, majoring in Social Science. Jocelyn found the college life to be quite interesting, especially at Fredonia State.

At Fredonia, the small diverse group of African American students quickly bonded to each other. Jocelyn's life took off in a whole new direction. Jocelyn met great people and became friends with a few, like Shinae, Kensala, Harmon and others. Jocelyn was changing, growing and learning to take life in strides.

Jocelyn and her roommate, Monica, a native of Brooklyn, New York got along well. Monica's West Indian descent made her accent immense, which drew interest among the people around her. Jocelyn's love for learning new things and learning about different cultures and people was profoundly evident when she met Monica. She felt drawn to Monica's highly excited and bubbly personality. Monica's outspoken personality made many of the Caucasian students at Fredonia feel threatened by her. Jocelyn felt Monica was simply misjudged.

The two roommates spent hours in nutty cackle sharing cheerful and lively talk. Monica dominated most of the talk, but that was okay with Jocelyn's calm and sweet demeanor. She enjoyed listening to Monica share her stories.

Prejudice and racism existed, but Jocelyn saw it from afar. Jocelyn's honesty, authenticity, and genuineness allowed her the freedom to treat all people with respect. Jocelyn got along well with her African American colleagues as well as her Caucasian colleagues. Interestingly, one of the Caucasian students felt comfortable enough with Jocelyn to say, "Jocelyn, you are okay. You are not like all the other blacks." Jocelyn wondered what she meant by that.

"All the other black students here seem to be hostile. They hover in one group in the student union as if plotting against us white people."

Jocelyn had an uncertain smile on her face. Her cheeks radiated with the flame of her spirit as she took the opportunity to enlighten her colleague. Jocelyn courageously explained that the thoughts this student had were far from reality.

"Trust me; the black students here at Fredonia are not interested in plotting and planning anything against the white students. The black students are here for an education, to get a degree and secure a well-paying job upon graduation."

Her colleague had a wide-eyed reverie look on her face.

"Okay. Your point is well taken."

"I guess I never thought...., well let's just say, I was taught to think differently."

"It is great we can have an honest dialogue about race."

Too often we misjudge people when we lack understanding and truth.

"Jocelyn, while we are being so open with each other, what are those long squiggly things that black people wear in their hair." Jocelyn boasted in a sudden bellow of laughter.

"They are called braids." Jocelyn was aware of her innocent motives and feelings. She respected her curiosity and appreciated that she asked questions. There were very few dull moments in Jocelyn's college experience.

One memorable day at Fredonia, Jocelyn's roommate Monica bolted in the room with an eager, almost greedy look on her face. She was on a high and couldn't wait to tell Jocelyn about the game she played with some of the Caucasian students she had become close with. The game, the *Ouija Board*. Monica explained with excitement how she contacted one of her dead relatives. She exclaimed, "Jocelyn, you have to see it for yourself to believe it." Jocelyn had always been a deeply spiritual person and the thought of contacting the dead unnerved her. The more Monica talked, the more the curious nature in Jocelyn kicked in. What could it hurt to watch, Jocelyn thought. She tagged along with Monica the next time she went to play the *Ouija Board*.

The room was lit only with flickering candles. The board unfolded and the alphabet scrolled across the panel with the words *yes* and *no,* one in each corner. Everyone participating placed their hands on a plastic triangle with the look of a glass eye. As the triangle began to move back and forth across the board, moving on its own, someone called out "Who is this? Can I talk to Uncle Fred?" The players asked the *"Spirit"* different questions. The questions led to either the *no* on the board or the *yes.* It spelled out messages with the letters engraved on the board. Jocelyn was not convinced it was real until she succumbed to a challenge by Monica to play. Reluctantly, she joined the game.

When she asked the board "Who is this?" the glass eye led the player's hands to the letters H-E-N-R-Y. Her sensitive spirit quivered and she jumped and squealed "Henry is my father's name!" The group shouted "Don't break the Trinity!" She secured her hands on the glass triangle.

"If you are my father, what is my mother's name?"

The group's hands moved to the letters K-A-T-I-E. Gentle tears slid down Jocelyn's face. For a moment, she believed she had found a way to connect with her father. The glass triangle jerked the hands of the players and desperately spelled out D-O-N-T - P-L-A-Y. Jocelyn never played the *Ouija board* again.

Jocelyn did not return to Fredonia after her first year. She planned to go back and finish, however, things in her life changed. She met and married Vernon and was now living the life of an Army wife. After Fort Bragg, North Carolina, Germany followed as their next duty station.

ALBERTA LAMPKINS

Sixteen

Unexpected surprise!

Vernon received military orders to a duty station in Germany in nineteen-ninety. Along with their one year old daughter, they packed up and off they went to explore a new country. Soon after they arrived, Jocelyn became pregnant with their son, Alex. The family made great friends with other military families stationed in Bamberg, Germany. Its beautiful architecture, pubs and romantically lit streets are adorable. The town has an old-fashion medieval appearance, which adds to its luster. The scenery and delightful pastries amazed Jocelyn and the sightseeing proved phenomenal. The family took part in traveling around Europe and purchasing some of the finest china and crystal in the region. For them, it was adventurous indulging in customs and traditions of a new place. However, even with all the adventures in another country, Jocelyn missed her family in Buffalo. She found it disappointing when she missed major family events. Like the one when she had to wait patiently to hear the news from back home by telephone.

Jocelyn nervously waited for the phone to ring. The sun filtered through the windows as she expected a call from her mother at any moment. She paced back and forth. She heard her son Alex stirring about in his crib and her daughter Audrey rumbling around in the room.

"Mommy." She went in their bedroom and got them up to eat breakfast.

She finished cleaning up after breakfast and giving her two children a bath. The phone rang.

"Hello," Jocelyn said with a subtle voice.

"It's a girl and she is beautiful and healthy," Katie announced with a jolly voice. The news thrilled Jocelyn!

To everyone's surprise, Jocelyn's oldest sister Alexandra had a baby. A baby girl she named

Nina. Alexandra was thirty-six. Everyone in the family had given up on the idea that Alexandra would ever be a mom, but she out witted them all. Katie was by her side every step of the way. With Katie and Nina's father's help, Alexandra did a good job being a first time mom. Jocelyn met her new niece the summer the family returned to the states.

It would be three years before Jocelyn, Alexandra, Marian, Bonnie, Henry Jr., Katie and all the grandchildren got together for a family reunion. Everyone got along well, including Alexandra and Marian and Marian and Bonnie. Food, fun, entertainment and love were present. It was Just like Henry Sr. would have wanted if he were alive; all his family members together. Katie blushed with delight. She made sure she had something special for every one of her grandchildren and they ate up her generosity and love like candy.

It was amazing to see Alexandra with her daughter, Nina. Nina was just three and she loved her mother. Alexandra would read bible stories to her and Nina sat on her lap and listened as if she was hearing her mother's last words. Nina also had a special bond with Katie, as all of Katie's grandchildren had with her. But there was something more meaningful with Nina.

Katie hated to see her children leave. One by one they went back to their own lives. Katie felt a cold, empty silence, the moment everyone left. She prayed, as she always did for each of her children to make a safe trip back home. Alexandra and Nina lived with Katie and were also sad to see everyone go.

Seventeen

Dear sister.

Death comes and leaves those behind feeling wounded and broken. Jocelyn had no idea when she last met with her family, it would be the last time she would ever see Alexandra alive. The smile that once triumphed, quickly became taunting.

Alexandra never liked going to the doctor. She self-medicated. She hoped one day to get stronger. She hoped to get better. Unfortunately, her life yielded to the inevitable and the battle ended. Cancer showed up and took over the whims of fate. Alexandra had a tumor that had lain dormant for years. The tumor caused her immense pain during her menstrual cycles. The growing tumor put an enormous amount of stress on her body. The severe headaches she experienced growing up and throughout her life were merely a trigger. Patient client privilege prevented Katie from knowing about Alexandra's cancer.

Most cancers develop slowly. It starts as a precancerous condition called dysplasia. It can be detected by a Pap smear and is usually one hundred percent treatable. Alexandra began developing severe symptoms such as fatigue, loss of appetite, pelvic pain and weight loss after she had Nina. Realizing her condition worsened and that she might not live to see Nina graduate from high school, Alexandra sought treatment. It was too late. The cancer had spread. She must have known what was coming. She tried to spend every waking moment she had with Nina. It was the happiest any of the family members had ever seen Alexandra. Jocelyn remembered the last words Alexandra said to the family when they gathered. It did not seem to mean much at the time. Alexandra announced, in a helpless voice with her lips twitched in a weak smile, "If anything ever happens to me, please take care of Nina." The family knew she was fragile, but had no idea how fragile.

The stars dimmed in darkness, as the family gathered to prepare for another loss. Katie waited until all four of her children arrived before telling Nina that her mother had passed away. Everyone in the family looked as if Christmas was canceled and New Year's passed them by. Katie, glad her children all arrived safely.

"Now that everyone is here. I'll tell Nina." Katie called Nina in the living room of her home.

She sat Nina down in a cushioned chair that sat alone by the fireplace. The tears that wouldn't stay still almost choked Katie. Katie pulled herself together. As she was about to speak, Nina grabbed Katie and hugged her neck.

"Don't cry, Granny. My mother has already talked to me."

Katie and her four children's mouths parted unexpectedly. Nina went on.

"My mother told me if she didn't come home, to put my hands together and pray. She is with Jesus."

A sudden wave of moans and sobs circulated between Katie, Marian, Bonnie, Henry Jr. and Jocelyn. Nina slid down out of the chair and courageously consoled her weeping aunts and uncle. Alexandra had prepared her three year old daughter for her passing. She had told Nina not to be sad when she left. The next day, after laying Alexandra to rest, Nina cried. The family cried with her.

Katie felt empty and joyless. She trained as a nurse to save lives. Cancer stopped by not once, but three times to let her know that only God can save a life. Cancer became a wicked and longtime enemy to Katie. She lost her mother to cancer. She lost her sister Jocelyn to cancer. She lost her child to cancer. The hurt showed visible in her eyes and the pain felt sharp in her heart.

The thought of going off somewhere alone and never speaking to the world again was tempting to Katie. Nina's bright and precious smile kept her going. It was difficult for Katie when Nina's father said that he was taking Nina to live with him. Heartbroken and sad, Katie had to trust that Nina would be okay. She was only minutes away if Nina needed her. She made sure Nina had everything that Alexandra would have wanted her to have.

After the passing of her sister, Jocelyn reflected upon her life. She was grateful for all her many blessings. She summarized that no one knows the day or the hour that their life may end. According to Jocelyn, people are placed in her life for a reason. And they are there as a part of God's plan in her life. All things, Jocelyn believed, work according to God's will. The imperfections she found in the people around her changed the day she lost her sister. Jocelyn now understood there are no perfect mothers, sisters, brothers and no perfect family. Love is unconditional and perfection is not required.

Eighteen

A Mother's heart .

The years passed by. Big Army moved Vernon, Jocelyn and their family from base to base across the country. After several moves, they returned to Fort Bragg, North Carolina for another tour of duty. Jocelyn's career as a patient advocate continued and took flight. She worked at Cape Fear Valley Medical Center and enjoyed her work off post. However, Fort Bragg, known for high troop deployments meant Vernon would be away a lot.

Katie, Jocelyn's mother, finally settled down. She moved to Oak Manor, a senior living apartment complex on Main Street in Buffalo, New York. Katie enjoyed living at Oak Manor and had made many friends. She talked about one lady she called "*Ms. C*" and shared how they looked out for each other. She also talked about being fond of Ms. C's daughter she called by the name "*Cat*."

Katie did well for a while, but soon her health declined and she could no longer live on her own. Katie's children were spread out and lived in different areas across the country. Moving with Jocelyn to North Carolina became the final decision among the family members. Katie did not want to leave Oak Manor, did not want to leave Buffalo and especially did not want to leave Nina. The adjustment went okay and Katie settled in with Jocelyn, Vernon, Audrey and Alex. Katie kept mentioning she wanted to write *Ms. C* and send her Jocelyn's address so they could keep in touch. She just never got around to writing *Ms. C*.

Jocelyn and her family were happy to have Katie come stay with them in North Carolina. For Audrey and Alex, it meant their Granny would spoil them and try to buy them whatever they wanted. Katie loved every one of her grandchildren. Like her grandmother stood up for her, so did Katie for her grandchildren.

Vernon prepared for combat in Iraq. He geared up to leave for the next twelve months. This was Vernon's second deployment in less than two years. No matter how much the family prepared, seeing Vernon off to war was never easy. So, having Katie there meant a lot to Jocelyn.

Katie's health progressively faded more than Jocelyn wanted to believe. The doctor diagnosed Katie with Congestive Heart Failure. She became too weak to care for herself. Jocelyn found her a good doctor in North Carolina and vowed that Katie would get better. Vernon did everything to make Katie comfortable in the rather large bonus room in the home. Vernon provided Katie with her own mini refrigerator, microwave and cable to watch all the Westerns, Judge Shows and football she wanted.

With Jocelyn's busy schedule as a Patient Advocate, she did her best to make sure Katie was comfortable living in North Carolina. The weather, however, was too hot for Katie's liking.

"You can put on extra clothes to stay warm in the winter or on cool summer nights in Buffalo. In North

Carolina you have to be almost naked to be comfortable! It's too hot! I'll take a cold Buffalo winter over a hot North Carolina any day!" Katie complained about the heat however, managed to enjoy spending time with her grandchildren.

Christmas would soon arrive and Nina, Marian, Bonnie, Henry Jr. and all of Katie's grandchildren were coming to spend Christmas in North Carolina with Katie. Katie made sure Jocelyn shopped for the things she wanted everyone to have. Jocelyn put up a Christmas tree in the bonus room for Katie. Katie had a hard time getting up and down the stairs without getting out of breath. The tree in the bonus room was more convenient.

Anna, Bonnie's daughter, arrived early with her son Devon, Katie's first great-grandchild. Jocelyn always had a good relationship with her nieces and nephews. It was common for one or two of them to spend time at Jocelyn's house. Just like her namesake, Jocelyn hailed as the favorite aunt of the family. Anna spent the most time visiting Jocelyn. Anna and Audrey, Jocelyn's daughter were close as cousins, despite their age difference of about seven years. Anna and Audrey share the same birthday causing them to have a special cousin bond. Anna helped to care for Katie along with Audrey and Alex. Nina's birthday fell three days before Christmas. As soon as Jocelyn got home from work, Katie insisted they call Nina to wish her a Happy Birthday. Jocelyn did as Katie asked and they called Nina. Nina missed Katie terribly and Katie missed her equally. Nina burst with excitement about coming to North Carolina to spend Christmas with Katie and the rest of the family. Katie held a heavy heart. She sat Jocelyn down in the room to talk.

"Jocelyn, I know I haven't been a perfect mother. And I know you never forgave me for not saving the house on Cayuga." Jocelyn listened attentively.

Katie went on. "There were a lot of things that happened in my life that I never talked to you all about."

Jocelyn twisted her body slightly and adjusted her back for comfort as she sat back further on the bed next to Katie.

"I have tried to protect all of you the best way I could. I lived for each of my children and grandchildren. I wanted you all to believe in the best that life had to offer. I never spoke ill of your father, because I know how much you loved him. But you have no idea the things we went through in our marriage. Life is not always as it seems. I learned that when I was a young girl. I grew up in a time in which you just accepted things for how they were. You never talked about it, and you never questioned."

Alex busted in the room.

"Granny, Audrey won't let me play the game you bought us."

"Wait a minute, your grandmother and I are talking, Alex." Jocelyn got the mother tone in her voice.

"It's okay, we can finish talking later. I know you have to get dinner started," Katie interjected. Anxious to address her grandson, she dismissed Jocelyn from the room and helped to resolve the issue between her grandchildren. Jocelyn went to start dinner.

After all the issues with her grandchildren were settled, Katie sat up in her burgundy recliner. She watched one of her favorite movies *The Color Purple*. She did not have an appetite and declined dinner. She said she was not hungry and just wanted to rest. Jocelyn left the room and closed her door.

In no more than an hour, Anna, Alex and Audrey screamed for Jocelyn to come help their grandmother. Katie had fallen on the floor and they could not help her get up. Jocelyn rushed to her and tried to help her up. Katie made a squeal that was frightening and went limp in Jocelyn's arms. Her last breath whistled like the wind in a keyhole. Jocelyn screamed for Audrey to call 9-1-1. The tears welled up and flowed abundantly.

The ambulance arrived. Jocelyn begged and pleaded with them to save her. Katie was gone. The stillness of finality hit Jocelyn. The paramedics refused to announce that they were unable to save Katie. They had Jocelyn and the family follow behind them in the ambulance. Once at the hospital, the doctor confirmed what Jocelyn already knew. Katie died on December twenty second, just before the night ended.

Marian, Bonnie and Henry Jr. were distraught. They arrived in North Carolina too late to see their mother before she passed away on up to heaven. No one expected Katie to be gone so soon. There is no love like a mother's love. Katie was gone, leaving her children to grieve her loss.

The family opened the presents she left them under her tree. Not a dry eye in the room. The family prepared her body for flight. Her body was shipped home to Buffalo. Katie was buried in Forest Lawn Cemetery with her husband Henry Sr.

Coping with loss is difficult. For Jocelyn, Marian, Bonnie and Henry Jr., adjusting to the loss of their mother stood in a field of its own. It counted as the most painful experience of their lives. Jocelyn believes there is a profound significance to the umbilical cord. The birth cord supplies the growing child with oxygen and nutrient-rich blood during the birth process. Yet, after the cord is cut, mother and child somehow remain connected. When her mother left the world, Jocelyn felt disconnected. Like she was now alone in the world. It's a feeling only someone who has lost their mother would understand.

Vernon arrived home from Iraq for the funeral services. The family comforted each other as best they could. Returning to North Carolina after the funeral proceedings was difficult for Jocelyn. She took her time going through some of Katie's belongings she left behind. Jocelyn cherished the notebooks with her writing and the phone book she used to keep everyone's number in. Katie had asked Jocelyn to get her a composition book. Katie wanted to write messages to her children and grandchildren. Before she could write a single message, she passed on. Jocelyn was sure she would have encouraged all of them to stick together as a family. Jocelyn held tight Katie's leather tote bag and put Katie's papers and phone book in the purse for safe keeping.

Nineteen

Is this a scam?

Family and friends all called to wish their condolences and check on the family. Jocelyn wasn't up for much talking and let most of the calls go to voice mail. When she finally scrolled through and listened to her messages, one message caused her to replay it several times. She was trying to make sure she heard what she thought she heard. The message said:

"Hi Jocelyn; this is Bobby, your mother's brother. I am sorry I missed the funeral. I just found out that Katie passed away. Please call me and let me know if there is anything that I can do for you or the family. My number is 276-555-555."

"What?" Jocelyn said out loud to herself.

The look on Jocelyn's face caused Vernon to stop flipping through the pile of mail from the mailbox.

"What's wrong with you, Jocelyn?" Vernon asked as he looked on with a peculiar look on his face.

"Listen to this message," Jocelyn asked.

Jocelyn played the message for Vernon to hear

"Your mother doesn't have a brother. Who is this person?" Vernon remarked.

"I have no idea. This must be some kind of scam," Jocelyn said and thinking how cruel for someone to play around. "The area code is a Martinsville area code. I'm not calling that man back. My mother does not have a brother," Jocelyn insisted. She called her sister, Bonnie.

"Hello, Bonnie. Guess what. I have a message on my phone from someone name, Bobby. He stated he was Mommy's brother." Jocelyn was eager to hear Bonnie's response.

"Mommy's brother? What?" Bonnie replied with the same peculiar tone as Jocelyn.

"Yeah, that is the same thing I said!"

Bonnie made a suggestion. "Let's call Aunt Lynette and ask her about this, but first let's call Marian and Henry Jr."

Marian and Henry Jr. were as confused about the message as Jocelyn and Bonnie. Jocelyn called her aunt Lynette after talking with her siblings.

"Hello, Aunt Lynette. How are you?" Jocelyn asked.

"I'm okay. I'm having a hard time with the loss of both my sisters," Aunt Lynette explained in a sympathetic voice.

Jocelyn explained to her aunt about the phone call she received from the mystery man named, Bobby. She told Aunt Lynette his call came from a Martinsville area code.

"This is crazy, right, Aunt Lynette?" Aunt Lynette hesitated and then said that Jocelyn should call him. "Why?" Jocelyn was surprised and confused by her aunt's response.

"Do you know him?" Jocelyn asked with defiance in her voice.

"No, I do not know who he is. Just call and see what he says. I'm curious," Aunt Lynette expressed in a calm tone.

She sensed Aunt Lynette knew more than she led on. She was too calm about this story.

...

Jocelyn dialed the number and called the mystery man, interested in learning what his motives were.

"Hello. May I speak to Bobby?"

A cheerful voice replied, "This is Bobby. This must be Jocelyn. I saw your number on the caller ID. I am glad you returned my call." Without hesitation he began saying how sorry he was to hear of Katie's death. Jocelyn listened, and then firmly stated:

"I don't know who you are. My mother does not have a brother. Who are you?"

"Oh," the mysterious man sighed. "She never told any of you about us," he said with hesitation and guilt. "I know all about you, your brother and sisters. I know when your oldest sister Alexandra passed away, and I know every duty station you and your husband Vernon were stationed at." Jocelyn was left speechless and without knowing what to say. The man continued the conversation.

"I just talked to your mother about a month ago. She told me she was living with you and your family."

"Do you know any of my mother's sisters?" Jocelyn finally found her words.

"Yes. I know your Aunt Jocelyn and your Aunt Lynette. It saddened me when your Aunt Jocelyn died."

Jocelyn was more confused than ever at this moment.

"Sir, I am startled by all this because I really have no idea who you are." Jocelyn's tone became friendly. Obviously, Bobby knew her mother.

"Do you know Janie Ruth?" the man asked.

"No, who is she?"

"Oh. I see. Maybe you should call Janie Ruth. Let me give you her number. She can explain all of this to you."

The man gave Jocelyn the number to the unknown lady. The area code for the number he gave her indicated it was also a Martinsville number. Jocelyn hung up from talking to the man and ran upstairs to the bonus room. She pulled out Katie's tote bag and reached for the phone book that she had stored in the bag. There it was, Bobby's address and number along with Janie Ruth's address name and number in Katie's personal phone book.

It was all too much for Jocelyn to handle at that time. She was still grieving and Vernon was leaving to finish his tour in Iraq. She saved the numbers and addresses to the man named Bobby and the lady named Janie Ruth. Her aunt Lynette assured her that she and her aunt Jocelyn were the only siblings Katie had. Something in Jocelyn's soul told her that it was more to the story, but Jocelyn let it go. She let it go for years, until now. She had to go to Martinsville to find out the truth.

Twenty

Keeping secrets.

*W*hat could I not know about my mother? Jocelyn posed the question in her mind. She had a desire to know and she set her mind in motion to find out. With the spirit of determination and curiosity, she took a deep breath in and then out. On the count of three, Jocelyn picked up the phone and dialed the number. She made the telephone connection with Janie Ruth.

Janie Ruth, according to Bobby, the mysterious man who laid claim to being Katie's brother, would have all the answers to Jocelyn's inquiries.

"Hello," Janie Ruth answered in a low tone.

"Hello. May I speak with Ms. Janie Ruth?" Jocelyn replied.

"Yes, this is Janie Ruth. May I ask who is calling?"

"My name is Jocelyn. My mother was Katie Harris," Jocelyn announced with hesitation.

"Oh my goodness. I am so glad to hear from you. I heard so much about you from Katie, when she was still with us. I miss talking to that girl," Janie Ruth said with a hint of sorrow in her voice.

"How are you doing, baby?" Janie Ruth ushered in before Jocelyn could speak.

"I'm doing well. I am calling because, well... after my mother passed, I received a call from a man named Bobby. Who-"

Before Jocelyn finished her sentence, Janie Ruth interjected.

"Oh, yes. Bobby," she said with assurance. "Bobby told me that he talked to you. He said you would call."

"Yes, ma'am. My mother never mentioned Bobby," Jocelyn remarked in a flat voice. "He said that he was my mother's brother. He did not say who you were in relation to her. He only said that you could explain."

"Yes, yes," the older woman replied in a matter-of-fact voice. "Katie kept our secret. Maybe, I should as well." Jocelyn wasn't convinced Janie Ruth wanted to keep her story a secret. She sensed she wanted to tell everything.

"Well, I have decided to make a visit to Martinsville. I haven't been there since I was a young girl. It would be gratifying to see the place one more time."

"Oh, baby, that would be so wonderful. I would love for you to visit. When are you planning to make your visit to town?" Janie Ruth replied with excitement and anticipation in her voice.

"Well, I booked a train ticket for next week. I thought I had better book it now before life got in the way and prevented me from making the trip."

"That's wonderful. I would love for you to visit with me when you arrive in town. I will share the truth when you arrive," Janie Ruth replied in a singsong tone of voice.

"I would like that very much. I have a lot of questions about my mother. It will be nice to meet you," Jocelyn replied with a mustard seed of relief.

"I have a great idea. Why don't you meet me at the Martinsville Historical Museum and Cultural Center? I will have the curator of the museum open the place up for us. I believe you will find everything you need there," Janie Ruth remarked.

"Okay. I am glad that I called and I am looking forward to meeting you and visiting the Martinsville museum."

Settled, Jocelyn trusted her own intuition and chose to take a curbed path to verify the accuracy of Bobby's statement. Jocelyn had to see the bigger picture. When she sets her mind to resolving an issue, she stopped at nothing to accomplish her mission. Besides, she was curious as to what story would unfold in Martinsville. She could hardly believe there was a story. A story involving Katie, her mother, baffled Jocelyn. She prepared for the train ride to Martinsville.

Twenty-One

A little Social Media.

An uncomfortably cool breeze on the train passed by in a hurry and Jocelyn felt the air on her neck, running through the train like a swift serpent. She pulled the rib of her collared shirt up closer to her chin and wrapped her arms around her body. Her hands flew in a vigorous motion up and down along the top end of her arms. It helped to stop the reflex shaking caused by the cold wind. Once she stopped trembling, she exerted a small amount of energy and reached for her iPhone from her purse. She checked all of her online social networking sites, her Facebook, Twitter and Instagram pages. She hit 'like" on a few of her Facebook friends' statuses and replied *yes* to attending the *Sister Circle Book Club Appreciation* event. Jocelyn joined the book club, founded by her friend Mary, when she lived in North Carolina. When Jocelyn left to move back to Buffalo Mary made her a "lifetime" member of the book club.

Jocelyn met Mary through her friend Alberta, who worked as a Caseworker and a Social Worker for the Cumberland County Department of Social Services (DSS). Alberta invited Jocelyn to join the book club. Jocelyn felt honored to be a member of the group. Mary and Alberta worked together at DSS along with Jo, Tracey, Verneyse (Pam), Alisha and Lawana (May she rest in peace). Jocelyn, Pamela, Billie, Karen, Keisha, Latricia, Lenora and Martha worked at other agencies in the area. As a member of the book club, Jocelyn got to meet the author Suzetta Perkins, whom she hopes will come visit one of the open mic nights at *Café Expressions*.

The connection with Alberta and the other DSS members was helpful for Jocelyn when she advocated for her clients at the hospital. Meeting new people and linking together with others was valuable in Jocelyn's profession. Alberta was a social butterfly and invited her to many different events during Jocelyn's time in

North Carolina. She got to know and befriend some of the people who Alberta regarded as good people. Phyllis, Bobbie, Danielle, Ms. Doris, Pam and Shannon worked at DSS with Jocelyn's friend Alberta; they became a valuable asset for helping Jocelyn meet the needs of the clients she served. There was no way Jocelyn would miss the appreciation ceremony celebrating *Sister Circle's* tenth year as a book club. Jocelyn made a comment with her acceptance to attend.

Looking forward to attending – Can't wait to see everyone. Miss you all!

Mary responded back almost instantly.

We can't wait to see you as well – glad you will be joining us! Are you attending the National Book Club Conference in Atlanta this year?

Jocelyn quickly responded:

Yes, I have already paid my deposit. It is another great line up of authors and publishers. Kimberla Lawson Roby, Eric Jerome Dickey, Hill Harper, Pearl Cleage and many others of my favorite writers. See you there as well!

The daily inspirational Facebook messages posted by Pastor Brian R. Thompson and his wife

Reverend Felica Thompson from Simon Temple AME Zion Church in Fayetteville were messages Jocelyn felt encouraged her. Even though she no longer lived in North Carolina to attend the church, social media allowed her to keep up with the things happening at Simon Temple. She also liked the fact she could continue to hear the awesome sermons given by Pastor Thompson via the live stream broadcast on the internet.

Social Media is awesome! Jocelyn proclaimed in her own mind.

Jocelyn hardly posted any photos or did any video sharing on Instagram, though her brother Henry Jr.'s two older girls always posted photos as well as her other nieces and nephews. Jocelyn kept up with how they are doing through Instagram.

She checked her Instagram; there were no new photos of her nieces and nephews. She checked her Twitter and scrolled through a few updates posted by Michael Baisden, a radio personality, producer, filmmaker, motivational speaker, social activist and author. Mr. Baisden tweeted:

Post the information and links to your music, book, film, or business. I want you to have a voice on my page to help you get closer to your dream. Please keep it clean, keep it short, and keep it classy – Michael Baisden

There were more than fifteen hundred likes and more than two hundred comments. Jocelyn decided to try her luck. She posted the link for her son Alex's music video titled *College and a Dream*. She tweeted then posted to Mr. Baisden's Facebook page:

Mr. Baisden, what a great opportunity you are giving people to showcase their talents and businesses! Please check out my son's music video on YouTube. Just type in College and a Dream and watch his awesome video.

The New York Times tweeted an interesting topic:

Republicans are proposing their own market-based solutions to poverty.

Wonder what that is all about? I'll have to go back and read that article later. Jocelyn posed the question and made a mental note to self.

Before she knew it the train conductor announced: "Train seven two seven will be making its final stop in Virginia. We should arrive on schedule at

10:15 am. Please prepare to exit the train and have your baggage claim ticket ready."

Jocelyn gathered her things, pulled out her baggage claim ticket from her purse and prepared for her arrival in Martinsville. The opening of the doors permitted Jocelyn to exit. Jocelyn's bags arrived and her attention was now on getting her rental car, getting to the Holiday Inn where she'd stayed as a child with her parents when they visited Martinsville and getting to the museum to meet with Ms. Janie Ruth.

She made a quick call to Vernon. "Hi, honey. I made it safely," she said in a jazzy kind of voice.

"Glad you made it safe. Call me when you get settled in at the hotel," Vernon replied, happy to hear that his wife made it there safely.

"Okay. I'll talk to you in a little bit. Love you!"

"Love you too."

It was partly sunny with a high temperature of fifty-five degrees outside. A family of birds was circling the sky in great lazy loops. Nestled in the foothills of the Blue Ridge Mountain, Martinsville had a distinctly hometown feeling. The people were friendly and went about their day in a semi care free manner. Jocelyn made her way to the hotel and put her things away and then drove around town for a bit before heading to the museum. Martinsville was as she remembered. The remarkable dirt resembling the hue of faded cherries sparked a distant memory of visiting the town when she was a young girl.

The Fayette Street Historic District where Katie's family once lived encompasses one hundred and sixteen contributing buildings, in a traditionally African American section of Martinsville. It included a variety of commercial, religious, educational and residential buildings dating from the late 19th century through the mid-20th century. Jocelyn felt a sense of connection to the little town and was glad she chose to make the trip.

ALBERTA LAMPKINS

Twenty-Two

This little town of mine, let it shine.

T he long bolts of hair threaded with silver helped to show the characteristics of Janie Ruth's age. Well refined in her conservative dress, Janie Ruth resembled a dignified school teacher of days past. Her small frame gave a few clues that she was once a thin, but shapely woman. Although she demonstrated with clarity the ability to recognize and draw fine distinction when she spoke, it took her a few seconds to gather her thoughts. The strong slender stick she used to help her walk gave her partially weak body stability as she stood to greet Jocelyn on the front porch of the museum.

"You are beautiful. Just like your mother!" Janie Ruth exclaimed in a slow and passionate voice. "Give me a hug," Janie Ruth demanded in a fragile voice as if she was going to cry.

Jocelyn gave Janie Ruth a graceful hug and smiled.

"I am so glad you came. You just don't know how much you made this old lady feel good. I know Katie would be glad you are here as well," Janie Ruth added.

Jocelyn wondered if that were true. Would Katie be glad that she was here talking to the lady she never mentioned to her children?

"I'm sure she would," Jocelyn replied in a honeyed voice as if she didn't really trust what she was saying.

"Jocelyn, this is Betty; she is the curator and overseer of this fine historical museum. She was kind enough to meet us here to show you around. There is a lot of history here in this museum." Janie Ruth spoke with slight hesitations after each sentence.

"Hello, Betty, it is a pleasure to meet you. Thank you for allowing me the opportunity to visit the museum." Jocelyn had a deep-seated curiosity.

Betty displayed an honest and unquestionable pride for the work with the museum. Through photos, public records and narratives from the townsfolk, the museum was like a walk back in time of the African American people, churches, social events, businesses and schools of Martinsville's past documented and housed in this small place on Fayette Street.

Befitting the honor, Betty opened the doors to the museum. Like a French painter unveiling his masterpiece, she had an approving smile with artistic elegance.

"Well, ladies, now that we have been formally introduced, shall we proceed on our journey?"

Her charming radiance and captivating speech was contagious.

"Yes, let's get started," Janie Ruth responded with a smile like dancing sunshine.

"Yes, please. I am very anxious to see what the museum has inside."

With growing anticipation, Jocelyn gave Betty a complimentary glance. Betty reached for Janie Ruth's hand and aided her on the guided tour. Although,

Janie Ruth visited the museum for its grand opening, she delighted in returning for another glance of a time preserved from her youth. The wrinkles that took notice to her face were more profound, but in an impressive way. Janie Ruth smiled and grabbed hold of Betty's arm.

The tour was off to a remarkable start. The endless wealth of resources displayed a multitude of facts. The curator was as familiar with the history as she was with the alphabet. The journey through the museum gave Jocelyn the feel that she had unlocked the door to world unseen by her before.

"Many great people, citizens and guests have moved along the path of Fayette Street. For those who did not get to witness our earlier black owned cafés, schools and businesses, we have put together a replica of what Fayette Street looked like in yester years. The time covers from the year 1905 to the present. The presence of African Americans in Martinsville dates back to 1619."

The hostess shared history of the first indentured servants to the town. Their roles played an invaluable mark in making Henry County a budding place for African Americans to thrive and survive.

Jocelyn was in awe. The museum was a replica of what the Fayette Street district looked like in days past. Jocelyn's full attention focused on the curator's oral and visual presentation. She was an astute observer, immovably silent as she listened and learned. The curator's voice was rich and vibrant like the middle notes of a bowed stringed instrument. The fantastic display and flowing imagery brought comforting reassurance of a time once revered.

"As the conditions requiring more help with tobacco production enlarged, the need for newly freedmen to work in the factories increased." Betty continued dispersing the information covering the next fifty years after the arrival of the blacks; who were inhumanely bound by contract for service.

The historical account of black churches, such as Mount Zion African Methodist Episcopal Church established in 1870, Beaver Creek Primitive Baptist Church established in 1878, High Street Baptist Church established in 1898 and Mount Zion United Holy

Church established in 1930 to name a few, were priceless memories of the town.

Jocelyn took note of her great-grandfather's name displayed as a once elder of Mount Zion United Holy Church. She beamed with pride. Like a bright window in a distant view, she saw what once was. In her mind, she saw a river of men and women walking through the streets.

Without warning, thoughts poured upon her soul.

Why did Mommy never take us to visit the church she grew up in? Why did she not share these notable heritages with us? And the questions in her mind went on.

"Are you ladies doing okay? Do you need to take a moment to rest, Janie Ruth?" Betty politely asked as a way to check the interest of her guests.

"Oh, I am just fine, just fine. I am okay with continuing. You are doing a fine job, Betty!" Janie Ruth responded.

"I am doing okay as well. My interest is peaked to the highest level and I am ready to continue on," exclaimed Jocelyn.

"Okay, then let's take a look at some of the schools and businesses that did our town a great justice," Betty remarked with a positive attitude. "Piedmont Christian Institute or PCI opened in 1923..." Betty carried on with sharing her knowledge about the beginning of all the black schools in Martinsville.

There were pictures of students from the school's beginning and Jocelyn marveled at the attire the children and young students wore during those times. She desperately searched to find Katie or her aunt Jocelyn or her aunt Lynette in the pictures. She did not find their faces among the groups in the pictures.

"As you can see, we had some impressive entrepreneurs who pooled their talents. They built parks, recreational centers and buildings that served the people of the community. Our black businesses consisted of barber shops, skating rinks, bowling alleys, cab stands and more." Betty went into further detail about the businesses.

The cab company started by Jocelyn's grandfather was listed as one of the distinguished businesses of that time. Jocelyn paused in reflection of the grandfather she never met, but whose business made a historical contribution.

Her whole soul wavered and shook. The beat of her heart was like a drum. A tear trickled down Jocelyn's face when she came across her father's name. Henry Sr.'s bowling alley shined among the legendary venues in Martinsville. She was the proudest of the proudest of daughters.

"Here we have..." Betty started, but quickly paused when she saw a look of distress on Jocelyn's face. "Are you okay?" Betty asked with concern in her voice.

Janie Ruth raised her eyebrows. Her dawning instincts fell into place.

"Umm, yes, yes. I am okay," Jocelyn proclaimed in an unbelievable tone.

Theories sprouted in her mind like mushrooms.

"You look like you just saw a ghost or something." Betty chuckled.

"No, no. I'm okay," Jocelyn insisted.

"Okay, here we go. Now in 1943, Martinsville…" Betty continued.

It drew her in as the moon draws water. Her naturally tranquil disposition was interrupted and Jocelyn knew she stumbled on to the truth. As clear as the parts of a tree in the morning sun, the truth was revealed.

"Now, ladies, I hope you have enjoyed our walk through time." Betty had an extra-ordinary gift of conversation. "Thank you for paying honor to the past residents of Martinsville's Fayette Street Historical District. I have a book that we have put together that highlights everything that you have seen today. We ask for a donation of twenty dollars for the book, a small price to pay for the detailed account of times past of Martinsville," the curator declared.

Jocelyn did not have to be sold. She quickly reached in her purse and paid Betty a total of eighty dollar for four copies. She knew Henry Jr., Bonnie and Marian would want the printed work of art.

Janie Ruth bought one book.

"I'll give this one to my great-granddaughter, Susan," Janie Ruth remarked with satisfaction. "Betty, I can't thank you enough for your hospitality. Every time I am here, I feel some kind of way."

Jocelyn thanked Betty for her consistent friendliness and energetic enthusiasm.

Betty gave Jocelyn her name and number on a business card. "Please call me if you or any one of your sisters or brother wants to take a visual guide through time. I will gladly open the museum for them. With the budget, we only open the museum on an appointment basis," Betty added.

All three of the ladies hugged each other before exiting the building.

"Jocelyn, how would you like to get some dinner at the Wild Magnolia Restaurant on Church Street? I believe you have some questions for me," Janie Ruth asked and ended with a confident fact.

"Yes, I have questions. Dinner at the Wild Magnolia sounds like a wonderful idea to me. I will drive us there."

The enriched experience stirred hazy recollections. Jocelyn's thoughts were as impatient as the wind.

ALBERTA LAMPKINS

Twenty-Three

The proof is in the picture.

An alert announcing a text message buzzed. Avoiding socially incorrect behavior, Jocelyn refused to acknowledge the automatic signal from her phone.

"Oh, Janie Ruth, may I have another minute of your time?" Betty interrupted Janie Ruth before getting positioned in the car.

"I forgot to tell you about the tickets for the upcoming dinner honoring Mrs. Ludie Hairston." Betty approached Janie Ruth on the sidewalk by Jocelyn's rented vehicle. The diversion gave Jocelyn the perfect opportunity to check her text messages. The first, a group message from her friend Tina addressed to Jocelyn and their friend Valencia. It read:

Hi, Jocelyn and Valencia, when you ladies get a chance, check your email. I have put together the itinerary for our girls' weekend in April here in DC. Let me know if there is anything else you would like me to add to our scheduled activities. Can't wait to see you two – can't believe we have not seen each other since our spouses were Army Recruiters in Chicago!

Jocelyn accomplished a rapid response:

Hi, Tina, I will check my email as soon as I return to Buffalo; I'm currently in Martinsville, VA. I know you have put together an awesome weekend for us. I can't wait to see you both as well! Oh, is there any way we can visit Pastor Jamal Bryant's church while we are in the area? Not sure how far the church is from where your new house is and I would love to hear one of his energizing sermons in person (smile). Talk to you soon!

Before Jocelyn could check the next scripted note, Janie Ruth motioned that she was ready.

"Thanks again, Betty!" Jocelyn gave her a final wave goodbye.

Jocelyn and her guest headed to Church Street with Janie Ruth directing the way.

Jocelyn cruised along the streets and monitored traffic in her rearview mirror. Janie Ruth pointed out different places that Jocelyn learned about at the museum. It was a lively discussion along the way.

They reached the venue. Jocelyn stopped curbside to let Janie Ruth out in front of the restaurant. A kind gentleman offered to help Janie Ruth from the car to the door of the restaurant and Janie Ruth waited in the lobby while Jocelyn parked the car. Jocelyn found a parking spot near the front entrance and walked a short distance.

The atmosphere felt lovely and quaint. Known in Martinsville for its variety of southern style cuisine, it was a good choice. The smell of freshly prepared food on the grill was inviting. The waiter escorted the pair to their table and scooted a chair out for Janie Ruth. She eased into her seat and prepared to place her order. The waiter explained the specials of the day as he placed a new set of utensils on the table.

"I'll have the Baked Penne Marinara and a glass of water with a slice of lemon," Janie Ruth instructed the waiter who was polite and ready to take orders.

Jocelyn scanned the menu. The Voodoo Chicken appeared to peak her interest, mostly because of its name. The entre consisted of fire grilled chicken basted with the Wild Magnolia's special sweet, yet spicy voodoo sauce over red jasmine rice accompanied by seasonal vegetables.

Interesting, Jocelyn thought, but settled on ordering the Blackened Tilapia Alfredo, a glass of sweet tea with lemon and a glass of water on the side.

In spite of the fantastic meal, deep pockets of query filled her mind.

The matter meant to be kept a secret, was now uncovered. The curtain opened and the truth was distinct as night and morning. Janie Ruth's well thought out plan was an excellent discernment. Without knowing it, the museum uncovered the blemishes of an extraordinary reputation.

Before striking a barrage of questions, Jocelyn waited for Janie Ruth to finish her meal. The pair exchanged casual conversation. Janie Ruth sensed Jocelyn's growing anticipation. Janie Ruth swallowed a sip of her water.

"I saw the expression on your face when you passed by the picture," Janie Ruth expressed with a pause at the end of her sentence. "I can tell you recognized the similarities in appearance." With a look of assurance Janie Ruth waited for a reaction.

"Yes, I did." Jocelyn shook her head in agreement. Grabbing her purse from the floor, she reached in and pulled the booklet from the museum.

Janie Ruth gazed at the picture. "Amazing how much she looks like him. We all used to say she resembled him the most. You got it. Dr. Anderson is your grandfather. Your mother and I are the daughters of our dearly departed town champion."

The pupils in Jocelyn's eyes widened and her eyebrows almost reached the edge of her hairline. She suspected. She was sure, but hearing it made it all the more real.

Flushed with victory, Janie Ruth explained that Dr. Anderson had influence in the town. His charm and magnetic personality was powerful and persuasive to the vulnerable women of Martinsville.

193

"His grace afforded him the opportunity to have a *special* relationship with women. To my knowledge, there are four of us sharing the same gene as dear Dr. Anderson." Janie Ruth thought for a second while counting names on her fingers. "There is Katie, Bobby, John and me. Your mother is my sister. That makes you my niece, Jocelyn!"

She felt a beautiful irony, cherishing a fallacy and exposing life's imperfections.

The truth had fallen like leaves on a driveway.

Bewilderment captured Jocelyn. A variety of conflicting and profound emotions surfaced. Jocelyn fell into a kind of confused astonishment.

"How did you all find out Dr. Anderson is your father? I mean did my mother know all along or is this something she found out later in life?"

Jocelyn had a million questions. Questions sounding like the continuous popping of corks poured out from Jocelyn.

"Slow down, baby," Janie Ruth remarked with a chuckle. "Let me explain." She sighed and then took a sip of her water then carried on.

"I believe everyone knew Katie was his child. She looked just like him. You saw the picture. He could not deny her if her wanted to. He would bring all four of us together when we were old enough to understand. He never came out and said that he was our father, but we all knew." Janie Ruth continued. "He was big on education. He made sure that we all attended college and graduated." She paused. "He, well… he helped our mothers see to our education." Janie Ruth ended her sentence to give Jocelyn the table for more questions.

"Did other people know? I mean did my grandmother ever talk to my mother about this situation? Did the man I thought was my grandfather, know of this information?" Jocelyn bombarded Janie Ruth with more questions.

"I'll put it this way, dear heart. That's just the way things were back in those days. Your mother kept our secret from you all. I guess because she wanted to protect the image of her mother. Maybe she did not want her children to feel tainted by the truth. Bobby just didn't know that Katie never told your brother and sisters about us. We are the *forgotten* children of the infamous, Dr. Anderson. Well, baby, I hope you found the answers you were looking for. Your mother loved all of you very much. Don't blame her for our past or our town *secret*," Janie Ruth concluded.

"I don't blame her. I am really glad that you took the time to talk with me and shared your story. This has been a memorable meeting. If it is okay, I would like to keep in touch with you... Aunt Janie Ruth." Jocelyn gave her a heartfelt smile.

"Oh yes, baby, that would mean a lot to me!" Her eyes sparkled like a star in the night.

"You know... your grandfather, Dr. Anderson, would be so proud of you. A college graduate with a master's degree. And the owner of a thriving coffee shop business. You have his entrepreneurial spirit for sure! I know Katie is proud up there!" Janie Ruth reached out and grabbed Jocelyn's hand. "You call your ole' Aunt Janie Ruth anytime you want!"

Stars were blossoming in the blackness of the night when the two ladies left the restaurant. With hearts full of joy, it was a pleasant ride to Janie Ruth's home. Jocelyn dropped her off and vowed to call her when she returned safely to Buffalo.

No sooner than Jocelyn could get in the door of her hotel room, her phone was buzzing. She had put her phone on silent to give Janie Ruth her full undivided attention during their get-together. She received four missed calls and two text messages from Vernon.

Her heart started pounding. She flushed with fear.

"Something must be wrong!" She threw her purse across the bed and immediately dialed Vernon. "Vernon, what's wrong!" Jocelyn almost screamed.

"It's your friend, Angel."

Jocelyn sensed an acute note of distress in his voice. "What's wrong with Angel?!" Jocelyn yelled.

"Angel is in the hospital. She tried to swallow a bottle of pills." Vernon came on out and said it.

"Oh my God, oh my God!" Tears formed like rain drops on her face. "Is she okay…is she okay?" Jocelyn repeated her question to Vernon, demanding he give her the answer of yes.

"I don't know, baby, the hospital will not give me any information. I just don't know right now."

Thoughts crowded through Jocelyn's mind. "I'll be on the next flight home!"

Twenty-Four

Face-to-face.

Wounded warriors come in all shapes, sizes and hues of color. Angel put her past on the top bookshelf, left it covered in dust and out of reach. It was a story she never wanted to read again. The terrible past lay afar, like a dream left behind in the night.

It was a dull grey morning. Angel rose from the warmth of her cozy full size bed and stumbled to put on her slippers and cotton robe. She made her way to peer out the window in her front room. The snow cascaded down, quickly adding inches. The sound of people scraping their windshields and shoveling their driveways was normal for this time of year in Buffalo. Men, women and children dressed in layers to shield themselves from the cold. Icicles formed and dripped from the roof of Angel's Italian style home.

Angel moved to the Allentown Historic District on the west side of town. She liked the charm and uniqueness of the area. It was one of the most culturally diverse neighborhoods in Buffalo. When the weather was warm, Angel enjoyed taking leisurely walks and admiring the Victorian style homes with the exquisite architectural features.

The Allentown Historic district, located in the heart of downtown and hotels, restaurants, art galleries and cultural venues were within walking distance of Angel's home. Angel never missed the annual Allentown Festival in June. Thousands of people from all around came to discover the creativity of different artists.

She picked her home based on her admiration for the low pitched roof, widely hanging eaves and tall narrow windows. It was a century old home with spectacular character and Angel believed she made a great choice.

Angel decided to work from home this day. She put some fresh wood in the fireplace and looked around her home. The transformation of her home impressed Angel. She picked the perfect wing back chair and decorative pillow to sit next to the fireplace. The comfy couch and love seat sat in a square shape outlining the Oriental rug made with earth colors. Angel had the original hardwood floors polished and restored, and they complimented the crown molding highlighted around the home.

Angel turned her master bedroom into her work room. Fabrics of all colors and styles filled the room, along with sketch boards, sewing machines, a cutting table, dress mannequins and other materials necessary to cultivate her creativity. Angel was gifted and simply able to imagine a design, fashion an entire outfit, and plan the accessories to match. Hat, handbags and jewelry all coordinated to bring her sketches to life. She preferred to work as a freelance designer working for one of the companies downtown as an independent contractor. She did not like to get too close to people – she did not trust easily.

She paid close attention to detail and her clothing arrangements made her marketable in the business. However, she only designed clothing for women and children and had no interest in a men's fashion line. Angel could earn a lot more money if she was flexible in this area.

The last drip of coffee fell into the twelve cup pot she had brewing and she poured herself a large cup. Someone in the company had the bright idea to buy Angel a Kuerig coffee maker and boxes of the k-cups in a variety of coffee flavors for Christmas. It was a great idea, with Kuerig being one of the number one coffee makers sold all over the world, but brewing one cup of coffee at a time was meaningless to Angel. The Kuerig sat in a box unopened.

Angel sank down on her couch with her coffee in hand. She reached for the remote control and turned on the television. She flipped through the channels and nothing took interest for Angel. She thought about calling her mother, but decided against it.

"Mommy is probably watching television in the lounge with the ladies at her senior living apartment." Angel smiled with relief knowing that her mother was safe from harm.

Cecelia Medina's hair turned as harsh as tropical grass and gray as ashes. Her spirits sank like a stone when she left the Bronx twenty-six years earlier. With sadness in her soul, she found work as a seamstress to make ends meet in Buffalo. Her high school education and experience landed her a job at a local garment manufacturing company. The hours were long and the pay low. Adding finishing touches on garments, sewing buttons, mending, repairing and altering dresses filled the hours of her day.

Obscured beneath her age were the hidden pitfalls of her life. She chose to forget the abuse and dismiss her marriage to Carlito. Too afraid he would find her, she never filed for a divorce. Cecelia saved every other penny in a fund to send Angel to Design school. If she could not save herself from the past, she wanted to save Angel. Out of sight, out of mind was her motto. Angel didn't talk about her life in the Bronx and neither did Cecelia.

Years of working with her hands caused a deforming disability. Unable to work any longer, Cecelia moved in Oak Manor, a Senior Living facility. Angel felt comfortable with Cecelia having access to twenty-four hour care. The senior living facility was safe and secure. Cecelia made friends at the home with Ms. Kay, and after years of pain, she found a bit of peace.

...

The doorbell rang and when Angel opened the door she thought she was dreaming. Then she remembered her father's voice and found it to be unnerving, inspiring fear.

"Angel Baby," Carlito Medina said as he stood face to face with Angel in the doorway of her home.

Angel stood frozen, as she did twenty-six years ago. The last time she watched him wage war against her mother.

"Angel Baby, it's me. It's your father. I finally found you, Angel Baby," Carlito said with a look of cynical joy on his face.

Before her stood a terrifying specter. Her face tightened like a mask.

Angel slammed the door and tried to forget seeing him.

"Angel!" Carlito shouted as he pounded on her door. "I have changed, Angel Baby. I've changed!" He insisted Angel knew that. "I came all this way to see you and to see your mother, ANGEL!" He proceeded to knock on the door in a succession of two or three hard poundings.

"Angel Baby, open the door," he said in a whimpering voice.

Angel remained hidden behind the door. She wished she was invisible as she stood paralyzed by fear.

"ANGEL, DON'T BE STUPID LIKE YOUR STUPID MOTHER. SHE IS THE ONE THAT TURNED YOU AGAINST ME!" Carlito shouted and pounded his fist against the wooden barrier.

It had become a pulse pounding event. Angel saw disaster like a ghostly figure following her. It set her memories humming like a hive of bees. A sudden sense of fear ran through her nerves like the chill of an icy wind.

"YOU TURNED OUT TO BE CRAZY AND STUPID, JUST LIKE YOUR MOTHER!"

His words packed an unwelcome punch and he knew immediately, it was the wrong choice of language. He continued the unbroken habit of a lifetime. He was bounded by the narrow fences of life. Heavy was his heart like stone.

As he prepared to leave, he knew the destruction he caused his family was irredeemable.

"Angel Baby," he cried out.

Suddenly, like death, the truth flashed by Carlito. His final words snapped like a whip-lash. He walked away somewhat unsteady like a blind man feeling his way. The sound of snow crunching underfoot faded with each step.

The world is as bitter as a tear.

Angel realized that her life was a lie and her father was the same monster. A bewildering sense of disbelief swept over her and she thought maybe she didn't deserve to live.

Her heart sped up faster when she thought she heard his voice again. She exhaled and thought about his last words to her, that day, that day she thought she would never see him again.

"Your mother is just stupid and she makes me do these things to her, Angel Baby."

Bitterness crept up and took control. She was left feeling like a lost bird in an empty nest. She saw it only as an omen full of possible danger.

Angel recognized he was gone and she was alone. She made one final call to her mother and left a voice message:

'He is here, Mommy, he found us.' Pause.
'I can't go through life anymore knowing he has found us. I can't take seeing you hurt again. I can't live in this world with him.' Pause.
'Good Bye, Mommy. I love you.'
Click.

Angel took the pills and wanted to die.

Her mother got the message and immediately called the police. When the police arrived Angel was unconscious, but still breathing.

...

Dr. Singer, head of Psychiatry at Buffalo General Hospital, requested a full background history on Angel Catalina Medina. Before talking to her and making a final diagnosis, he studied and paid close attention to the details in the case history he received from Child Protective Services (CPS) Loveless County Department of Social Services.

The report read:

Loveless County Department of Social Service

Child Protective Services Case Summary Report

Type of Report: Initial

Date of Report: May 16, 1989

Source of Report: Intake Social Worker

Date of Initial Contact: May 16, 1989

Current Allegation: Injurious Environment

Mother: Cecelia Medina, age 28

Father: Carlito Medina, age 33

Child: Angel Catalina Medina, age 8

(No other members of the Household)

Allegation Summary:

Mrs. Medina admitted to the County hospital and treated for a severe head injury and other injuries sustained from multiple beatings inflicted upon her by her spouse. She was accompanied by her 8 year old daughter, Angel, who was present in the home while Mrs. Medina and her spouse were in a domestic altercation. Angel was not injured during the altercation, however, displays the characteristics of being emotionally distraught.

Mr. Medina fled the home when a neighbor called the police to report hearing screaming from the home. The whereabouts of Mr. Medina are unknown. Mrs. Medina gave Social Worker permission to place Angel in kinship care with her sister, Susan, until safety for Mrs. Medina and Angel can be further assessed.

Family Background:

Mother - Cecelia Medina is a 28 year old Caucasian female who has been employed as a seamstress and dressmaker for the past five years. She earns about $28,000 a year. She has been married to Carlito Medina, a Hispanic male age 33 for eight years. They have one child, Angel age 8. Mr. Medina is employed in the construction business and his annual earnings are unknown. Cecelia, Carlito and Angel are all U. S. citizens residing in Loveless County for the past eight years.

There have been four prior reports of domestic violence incidents between Mr. and Mrs. Medina in which their daughter Angel was present during all four altercations.

Mrs. Medina has a history of abuse as a child; she is diagnosed with depression and post-traumatic stress disorder. Mrs. Medina was being treated for depression and anxiety, however, she has stated that she has not been to see her therapist in over a year and a half. She has one sister who lives in the area.

Mr. Medina has a history of irrational and erratic behavior. He is diagnosed with an anger disorder and alcohol abuse. He has repeatedly refused treatment and denies that his alcohol use is excessive. He has maintained stable employment as a sub-contractor for several local construction companies. Mr. Medina has no close relatives in the area.

Angel Catalina Medina attends Briar Elementary School and is in the 3rd grade. School records report that she is doing well in all subjects in school and is a pleasant child in class. Previous case record reports that Angel has a close relationship with her mother, Cecelia, and fears her father, Carlito. Angel often spends time helping her mother putting clothing patterns together, matching threads and fabrics.

Cecelia Medina's Account of Allegation:

Mrs. Medina stated her husband Carlito inflicted bruises and caused a slight head trauma to her in the presence of her eight year old daughter Angel. She stated she and her daughter were working on a dress pattern in the spare room she uses for sewing and did not realize the time. She stated she was late preparing dinner and the food was not ready when her husband arrived home.

She stated that he became upset and angry and said "You stupid woman, I have been working outside in the cold weather all day and I am hungry. I'm tired of you messing around with those stupid dress patterns and not having my food ready when I get home." Mrs.

Medina stated she told him that dinner would be ready in the next ten minutes. She stated her daughter ran to set the dinner plates on the table to show her father the food was almost ready.

Mrs. Medina stated she could tell he had already been drinking and could smell the alcohol on his breath. She stated he grabbed her arm and pushed her towards the refrigerator in the kitchen. She stated her head hit the corner of the refrigerator and she saw blood. She stated that he then shoved her to the floor and began punching her repeatedly.

She said her daughter Angel stood frozen and before she knew it, she felt herself about to black out. She stated a neighbor or someone must have called the police when they heard her screaming.

Mrs. Medina stated before the police could arrive, Mr. Medina left the home and she has not had any further contact with him. She stated the police called the paramedics and she was taken to the hospital. She stated she was unable to get in touch with her sister at the time and her daughter Angel rode along with her in the ambulance to the hospital. She stated she left a message for her sister to meet her at the hospital. Her sister, Susan, arrived and is currently caring for her daughter Angel.

Social Worker did not observe any visible marks or bruises on Angel. Social Worker observed Angel to be in good physical health, but frightened and afraid to talk about what she witnessed. Social Worker did not pressure Angel into telling her story.

Social Worker recommends that Mrs. Medina attend domestic violence counseling, individual counseling and parenting classes. Social Worker also recommends counseling therapy for Angel.

Safety Plan:

Social Worker discussed safety plans with Mrs. Medina. Social Worker recommended that Mrs. Medina gather all her vital documents in one safe place, pack a change of clothes for her and her daughter Angel, have sufficient cash available in case she has to leave in a hurry, and identify a place she can go unknown to her husband.

Mrs. Medina agreed to this safety plan and stated she will request help from her sister to be a safety resource for her and her daughter. Mrs. Medina stated she is considering relocating to a new city to get away from Mr. Medina. Mrs. Medina agreed to insure the safety of Angel.

Twenty-Five

Broken souls leave deep wounds.

She confessed everything and thought maybe she could save Angel from all the pain and turmoil she and Carlito caused her. Cecelia admitted she was swollen in a state of dishonor and did not have the spirit to face her situation. She endured a repeated sequence of ill-treatment and misery. Not only at the hands of her husband, but also at the hands of her father and her mother when she was a child.

"The Cycle of Abuse." Cecelia called it as tears marched down her face in a slow but steady stream.

She witnessed life as an entity created to dominate her rather than life being something she could come to terms with and deal with successfully.

"That's the way life is," is how Cecelia explained what she had been through over the course of her thirty-four years in the world.

She felt weak and not strong enough to withstand the shock of her daily experiences. One of the inherent concerns of the "Cycle of Abuse," is that many people like Cecelia, are in a repeated sequence of events that develop into problems and habits. The cycle destroys their emotional health, physical health, and demolishes their self-worth.

Diverting her problems to the farthest side of her mind and tucking them away was a skill she mastered as a child. Cecelia was not able to comprehend the seriousness of her revolving cycle of destruction. Her mental state characterized a sense of inadequacy and feelings of gloom. Her unsatisfactory personal belief in herself and the absence of courage to fight against her hostile environments caused far-reaching damage.

For more than eight years with no relief, Cecelia came to the defense of her husband's offensive behavior. He took advantage of her weak and fragile state of being. He expected her to "take it" and he expected her to cower down to his selfish needs and desire to be in control. He poured bitter and biting ridicule on his weak opponents.

Affected by a turbulent and unruly childhood, Carlito fell victim of his own circumstances. His father was an alcoholic and his mother took out her frustrations with his father out on Carlito. His mother was the abuser in his household. His father drank to drown out his mother's aggressive control over the family. Carlito, a victim of the ugly wheel of wayward behavior. It had become an unbroken habit of a lifetime.

Carlito's overbearing pride and his superiority toward Cecelia was a disguise to mask his own low self-respect and worth. He fell right into the trap and never tried to get out. The liquor and brew that he repeatedly swallowed, enhanced his rebellious nature and caused him physical, moral and emotional ruin. The gin was cheap, but to Carlito the intoxicating feeling he received after the fourth or fifth shot was worth it.   It numbed his feelings of intense unhappiness and state of misfortune.

How could two severely dysfunctional people marry?   The pamphlet on the *Tips for a successful marriage or relationship* never reached Cecelia and Carlito Medina.

1.   Get to know and learn about each other.

2.   Love, respect and honor one another.

3.   Communicate with each other in a positive manner to promote peace in the home and not war.

4.   Take time to listen and not be defensive.

5.   Support each other and never criticize or judge harshly.

6.   Never physically, mentally or verbally abuse one another.

Maybe if someone had told them that the pre-requisite before entering in a relationship is:

First have *Self-Love,* life for Cecelia and Carlito would have been different.

The trauma of being an unwanted spectator for the disadvantaged boxing match between her parents left Angel deathly afraid of Carlito. He knew it; he finally saw it, before he ran off in hiding. The look of terror in Angel's eyes reached the soul of her mother. Cecelia finally decided she would no longer put herself or her daughter in harm's way. In her fear of further hurting Angel, she gathered all her scattered impulses into one single act of courage. In the still of the night, Cecelia, Angel and Susan, Cecelia's sister, left the Bronx and moved to Buffalo, New York. Angel was eight years old and never wanted to view her father's face ever again.

…

After thoroughly reading the notes from Angel's past, he prepared to visit with his new patient. Dr. Singer knew that oftentimes, you have to understand a person's past before you can address their present.

It was not easy for Angel to open up to Dr. Singer initially. He built a rapport with her. And when she finally reached a turning point, her heart sang the song of freedom as she unleashed her words to Dr. Singer. A caged bird set free. A river of tears escaped down her face and settled on the many pieces of tissues that now filled her lap.

For more than twenty-six years, Angel never shared her side of the story. She never talked about her father or how she felt or what her past meant to her. She buried her past deep under the surface and hoped that it would never see the light of day. Angel thought about suicide in the past, but never thought she would try it.

Dr. Singer allowed her the time to talk. He asked Angel a series of questions related to her health. He jotted down a series of notes as she willingly spoke. Something about Dr. Singer made Angel feel safe. Dr. Singer promised to check back in on Angel before he left to make other rounds in the hospital.

When Dr. Singer returned to his office, he typed up his evaluation and made a diagnosis on Angel's case. The report read:

Physician's Report and Evaluation

Angel Catalina Medina: brown eyes, long brown hair, petite in size, is a fashion design school graduate. She moved from Bronx, New York to Buffalo, New York when she was eight years old. She is the only child born to her parents. She suffers from the long term effects of abusive behavior from her father. Alcoholism and Domestic Violence plagued her life and caused her to be unable to form long-term healthy relationships built on trust. Her fear based esteem issues hamper her ability to form bonds with primarily people of the opposite sex.

She observed the aftermath of violence between her parents; the blood, the bruises, torn clothing and broken furniture and other broken items. She has a history of always being on guard, watching and waiting for the next inappropriate incident to occur in her life. She never knew what triggered her father's anger towards her mother and therefore she has never really felt safe. She worried about her own safety, as well as the safety of her mother. She felt powerless.

Never was Angel struck by her father, but his behavior towards her mother weakened her heart by the war he waged against her mother. She had a strong regard of affection for her mother, though her mother lacked the ability to shield herself from the danger inflicted upon her by Angel's father. Both Angel and her mother were victims of her father's abusive behavior.

Angel kept the family secret, remained silent and never talked to her mother or anyone about the abuse between her parents. She was lead to believe that she should look as if everything is fine on the outside and hide the terrible pain she felt for herself and for her mother on the inside. Her home life was chaotic and crazy and she blamed herself for the abuse happening between her parents. Angel thought that if she had not done or said a particular thing that the abuse may not have occurred. These were her memories as a child.

Feelings of embarrassment and humiliation over ran her mind and she felt isolated and vulnerable. She wanted attention, affection and approval from both her mother and her father. Because her mother struggled to survive, she emotionally abandoned Angel without realizing what she was doing.

Because her father was consumed with controlling everyone in the household, he also emotionally deserted Angel. As a result, fear, guilt, shame, depression and anger towards her father took over replacing any trace of love she may have had for him. Angel felt denied the kind of home life that fostered a healthy relationship and healthy development as a woman.

Putting Angel's mother down and calling her "crazy" and "stupid," was the loveless language used by her father. He never once told Angel that he loved her. He seemed to have been incapable of expressing love in a positive manner. Angel's father did not supply the feelings of warmth, closeness and other good feelings of family. Coffee produces the good feelings Angel seeks.

Diagnosis: **Post Traumatic Stress Disorder (PTSD)**. PTSD is a mental health condition that is triggered by a terrifying event. The symptoms may include: flash backs, nightmares and severe anxiety, as well as uncontrollable thoughts about the event or events that occurred. PTSD may shake up one's whole life.

Diagnosis 2: Secondary Trauma Disorder (STS). The condition characterized by individuals who hear or see firsthand traumatic experiences of another. Its symptoms mimic those of post-traumatic stress disorder (PTSD). Accordingly, individuals affected by secondary trauma may find themselves re-experiencing personal trauma or notice an increase in avoidance reactions related to the indirect trauma exposure. They may also experience changes in memory and perception; alterations in their sense of self-efficacy; a depletion of personal resources; and disruption in their perceptions of safety, trust, and independence.

Twenty-Six

Faith, Friendship and Recovery.

Jocelyn caught the first flight back to Buffalo. Vernon picked her up from the airport and drove her straight to the hospital.

"I'm here to see Angel Medina, please."

"She is in room 807-A. Take the elevators to the left and see the receptionist at the desk when you get up there."

"Okay, thank you." Jocelyn walked at a fast pace to reach the elevators. "I am here to see Angel Medina."

"She is resting, but I will let her know you are here. What is your name, ma'am?" the nurse said in a pleasant voice.

"I am her friend, Jocelyn."

Jocelyn paced back and forth in the waiting area until the nurse gave her the okay to go in to see Angel.

"Hey, girl, how are you doing?" Jocelyn asked as she tried to remain calm.

"I could use a cup of coffee." Angel laughed.

"I am glad to see you." Angel lowered her gaze as she felt her heart sink.

"I'm glad to see you too." Jocelyn paused and then continued her conversation with hesitation in her voice. "What happened, friend?" Jocelyn was sympathetic and concerned. She didn't want to press her against her will.

"You know how they have all these different color ribbons for different causes."

"Yes," Jocelyn replied with interest.

"Well, I think they should have a ribbon made with multiple colors. Each new color woven together to represent a survivor of more than one cause. Mine would represent Domestic Violence, Troubled Childhood and Post Traumatic Stress. I guess PTSD is not only a diagnosis for soldiers coming back from combat. It is also a diagnosis for children who saw severe abuse of their mother."

Angel poured her heart out like a poet writing her first verse. Her words sounding like wavelets on a winter shore. Her upbringing was like a ship tossed to and fro on the waves of life's sea and she finally settled her thoughts.

"I never went to counseling or anything," Angel said with regret. "My mother still had a hard time talking about our past and wanted us to forget what once was." Angel went on to tell her story.

"The mental health professional assigned to talk to me has recommended counseling. He said I have suffered through a battle and it is time to heal."

"I agree, Angel." Jocelyn gave Angel a heartfelt hug.

"I have been full of misery for so long, that I believed I was okay. Seeing my father again caused me great distress. I had an imperfect understanding of my life. I felt like my mother was not strong enough to protect her own self. She was unable to shield me from witnessing her danger."

Jocelyn allowed Angel to talk to her as much as she wanted. She listened with an empathetic ear and her heart went out to Angel.

"You know, Jocelyn, I have never shared my story with anyone. There is something special about you. Thank you for being a friend. I feel we somehow have a connection to each other."

"Isn't it amazing how God works? If Vernon and I had not decided to move back to Buffalo and open our café, I would have never met you."

"God has a way of delivering the right people in the right place at the right time."

"So, here I am. And, I will be here for you."

"Just let me know what you need," Jocelyn said with a smile.

"Coffee, lots of coffee!" Angel laughed a hearty and joyous laugh.

"Now, tell me all about your trip to Martinsville. Did you find out who that man was?" Angel was ready to move past her situation and hear all about Jocelyn's trip.

Jocelyn spent another twenty minutes telling Angel about the trip and what she discovered.

"Wow, I'd rather have your family secrets than mine," Angel said as she regressed back for a moment on the thought of seeing her father.

Just then, the nurse came in to check on Angel.

"Oh my God, Peaches!" the nurse squealed when she saw Jocelyn.

"Raquel W., how are you doing, girl?! Jocelyn replied with excitement.

"Ms. Medina, I am so sorry. I didn't mean to be unprofessional. Peaches and I went to Grover Cleveland High School together and were good friends," the nurse explained.

"Wait a minute. *Peaches*, Jocelyn, your name is *Peaches*?" Angel had a quizzical look on her face.

Jocelyn giggled.

"Yes, that's my nickname. My father gave my brother and sisters each a nickname. He named me, Peaches. My family and close friends from Buffalo still call me by my nickname," Jocelyn explained.

"Your mother is Ms. Kay! Ms. Kay, from Oak Manor!" Angel couldn't believe it. She had a feeling she somehow knew Jocelyn.

"Your mother lived at Oak Manor, where my mother lives. Ms. Kay looked out for my mother and made sure no one took advantage of my mom. I loved your mother - she was good to me and treated me like family! My mother and I knew she moved to North Carolina with the daughter she called, Peaches, but I didn't connect it until now."

"Oh, wow. You knew my mom. This is unbelievable! "

"I guess we were really meant to meet each other."

Raquel, Angel's nurse and Jocelyn's high school friend chimed in and explained how she knew Ms. Katie as well. Raquel and Angel expressed their sympathy for the loss of Jocelyn's mother.

Just then the doctor arrived. He stood tall, lean, brown and handsome. Raquel talked briefly with the doctor then said her goodbyes to Angel and

Jocelyn. She wrote her phone number on a sticky note and gave it to Jocelyn to call her.

"How is my patient doing today?" Dr. Singer spoke in a casual, yet caring voice.

"Much better, Dr."

Angel introduced Dr. Singer to her friend. Dr. Singer expressed his gratitude to meet Jocelyn and asked if Jocelyn would be willing to be a safety resource for Angel.

"Ms. Medina told me all about you and your café. She thinks very highly of you and I think it will be good for her to have you as a resource."

"Yes, I will be here for her. Whatever she needs, I am willing to help."

The doctor left the hospital room.

"He is cute. I think I am going to enjoy therapy." The two ladies giggled.

"I have to get ready to go, but I just remembered something. Something my aunt Jocelyn, shared with me as a young girl."

Jocelyn told Angel about the message her aunt gave her about how to handle challenging moments. She explained her aunt told her there would be difficult times in life and things will happen. And we won't understand why. She told her that her aunt said when difficult days come, lift your head up high, and ask God to give you the strength to fly. The strength to fly past all those things, which only God has the answers to.

Remembering those words sent a rush of emotions through Jocelyn and Angel. Jocelyn understood what her aunt tried to teach her. Both Jocelyn and Angel's minds rested on those words as two chasing butterflies might rest together on a flower. Jocelyn prayed with her friend and left feeling lifted.

The words of the wise fall like the tolling of sweet grave bells upon the soul. A sense of infinite peace brooded over the hospital room where two friends shared a moment of hope. A week or so passed before an end to Angel's past settled.

...

Angel's father met her mother face to face and he apologized for the trouble he caused his family. He returned to the Bronx and signed up for counseling. His therapist suggested he write Angel and her mother a letter expressing his feelings. He wrote:

Dear Cecelia and Angel,

I know I cannot change what has happened in the past. I want you to know I am sorry for hurting the both of you. Maybe one day you can forgive me.

Signed,

Carlito

Medina

Angel clutched the letter in her hand. She prayed and asked God to help her learn to forgive.

…

A few days passed. Angel combed through her Facebook page, a quote written by Iyanla Vanzant., the famous motivational speaker and life coach, stood out. The words transformed Angel. It read:

"Forgiveness requires Surrender."

In that moment, Angel agreed to stop fighting, hiding and resisting. She granted herself relief from her pain and gave herself permission to be happy despite what life dealt her.   Forgiveness does not change the past, but it enlarges the future.

Twenty-Seven

Poetic Justice.

With all that happened with Angel, Jocelyn finally got a chance to sit down with her siblings to share what she learned in Martinsville. Henry Jr., Bonnie and Marian were shocked and amazed with the story. Neither of them could believe that Katie never shared a bit of this information with her children.

Unfortunately, the facts Janie Ruth presented to Jocelyn about Katie being the child of Dr. Anderson, would remain just a story. The siblings had no way to prove they were *heirs*, to the Anderson estate.

"I guess that's the way Momma wanted it." Marian attempted to justify the situation.

Jocelyn expressed how saddened she was to see that the *Colored People's* cemetery where their grandparents were buried was overgrown and unrecognizable. The siblings planned to return to Martinsville together and clean up their family's plots. Jocelyn gave her siblings a copy of the book from the museum. Each treasured the history presented in the book.

Thinking about Angel's story made Jocelyn realize the magnitude of what it means to forgive. She summarized, that although her family was nowhere near perfect, both her parents, Henry and Katie, did their best to love Alexandra, Marian, Bonnie, Henry Jr. and Jocelyn as they knew. Life doesn't always come with instructions. Learning to forgive yourself and learning to forgive others frees your soul, according to Jocelyn.

Jocelyn ended the meeting with Henry Jr., Marian and Bonnie to prepare for an elite evening at the café. It was open mic night and Jocelyn and Vernon worked hard to promote the event. They were expecting an impressive crowd and Jocelyn wanted to make sure everything was perfect. Jocelyn invited her siblings to return for the occasion.

Cool jazz, relaxed tempos and soft variants of bebop drifted through *Café Expressions*. Jocelyn and Vernon were busy preparing for open mic night. Vernon mingled with the band, did sound checks for the microphones and went over instructions for the evening with the master of ceremonies. Jocelyn hustled about insuring the atmosphere had an inviting feel in the venue.

Dimly lit candles flickered on the round tables dressed in black table cloths. Artful paintings and pictures of jazz legends lined the walls. Selected poems created by visitors to the café, were framed and put on display. Poems written by some of Jocelyn favorite poets like Langston, Maya, Giovanni, Sanchez and Mahubuti also found a home at the Café Expressions.

The low ceilings helped fill the place up with sound; you could hear every instrument distinctly. The nice acoustics were pleasing to their patrons. The tables surrounded the front of the platform for artists, creating an elegant and intimate atmosphere.

The spacious room was inviting for guests coming to hear original spoken words, music and comedy. Jocelyn and Vernon put together a savvy mix of imagination and hard work to build their business. Sophistication, energy and style made Café Expressions a welcoming, peaceful and friendly place.

This particular evening at the café had a special something in the air. Jocelyn's siblings, Henry, Bonnie and Marian came out early to support Jocelyn and Vernon and to get a good seat. Their daughter Audrey and son Alex were also present for the open mic night. Tasha, Jocelyn's lifetime friend made an appearance for the show. And to their surprise, Jocelyn's sister/friend Zena flew in from Warner Robbins Air Force Base to support the open mic extravaganza. Simona, Jocelyn's friend from Fayetteville stunned her as well when she arrived. Jocelyn felt invigorated by the overwhelming support of her friends. The evening was off to a great start.

The doors of the café opened and local talent signed up on the list for their turn at the mic. Jocelyn and Vernon hired a DJ to set the mood and keep the atmosphere buzzing with energy. There were lively conversations before the readers began their performance. Food and drinks were served and the master of ceremonies opened the floor with a joke.

"Hey, everybody, I have a question for you."

"How many ruined cars, bikes and motorcycles will it take for the city to fix the potholes in Buffalo?"

"I mean really. My grandmother can't even ride her motor scooter across the street without tipping over in a pothole."

The crowd bursts out in laughter.

"I mean really. Last summer she got stopped by the Buffalo police and received a ticket."

"I said 'Grandma, how you get a ticket from riding a motor scooter?' And you know what she said?"

"She said she got a ticket for leaving the scene of an accident."

"What accident, Grandma?"

"She said, Billy and I were riding our scooter to the store. I told Billy to swerve right and that sucka swerved left. He hit a pothole and got stuck in the street. I left his dumb butt there. Everybody knows you have to swerve and weave. They told us that when we got the scooters."

It was a lively opening.

The rhythmic percussions and the sound of jazz from the live band played an interlude before the next performer.

Jocelyn looked up and saw her faithful friend, Angel enter the café. She was glad to see her there and to her astonishment, Cecelia, Angel's mother was with her.

"Welcome to Café Expressions, Ms. Medina. We are delighted to have you here!"

Jocelyn showed all her pearly whites as she reached to give the frail woman a hug.

"I heard so much about your place from Angel, I had to come see for myself."

"Well, thank you for coming out tonight. I am going to get you a seat up front."

Cecelia gently grabbed Jocelyn's hand and held it in her palm.

"I want to thank you for what you have done to support my Angel. Ms. Kay, your mother did the same thing for me. Life has given us a hard blow. With people like you and your mother, the world is not so bad." Cecelia patted the top of Jocelyn's hand two times and then let it go.

"No problem. That's what friends are for. She is a blessing to me as well. I am glad you had an opportunity to meet my mother and that she was a good friend to you."

"I wish I had known she passed away, I would have been there. We had no idea how to reach her when she moved to your home in North Carolina. We didn't know." Cecelia felt sorrowful.

"It's okay – I'm sure she is looking down from above and smiling because we have all met and became friends. Not a day goes by that I don't miss her and wish I could talk to her."

"A mother's love is like no other."

Jocelyn fought back the tears lined up ready to march towards the corners of her eyes.

Miss you, Mommy, Jocelyn said silently in only her mind. "Now let's get you situated before the next performer, Ms. Medina!" The diversion tactic Jocelyn worked to prevent her from thinking too long about the loss of Katie.

Angel interrupted Jocelyn before she could dash off. "I want to read tonight."

"Wow, Really?"

Jocelyn felt amazed and excited about Angel's announcement. Angel had been to most of the open mic nights and never performed.

"Yes, I want to do it."

"Well, I am going to put your name on the list right now. I am looking forward to this!" Jocelyn scurried away to get the sign-up sheet. "Okay, you are number eleven. Our last act of the night!"

Local artists shared their verses and flows and showcased their amazing gifts for words and music. It was just how Jocelyn and Vernon imagined things to be. Self-expression is a powerful way to heal in Jocelyn's opinion.

Number eleven was up.

"Our next artist is a virgin to the mic. Let's give a warm welcome to Angel "Cat" Medina!"

The audience clapped and snapped their fingers in unison.

The hidden instinct of self-preservation kicked in. Angel made her way to the microphone and clutched her notebook tight in her hand. She paused for a second then gathered her composure. At first she appeared nervous. Then she relaxed and gazed in the direction of her mother.

The crowd came to a hush and fixed their thirsty eyes upon Angel.

Angel cleared her throat and read.

Coffee

It sat there
Nestled in my hands
Warming my heart
Filling me with a cup full of love
Rich and creamy
It takes the pain away
Pain is this to me
I saw it first hand

Through fists of fury
And a mother's hurry
To miss his back-hand

Weeping eyes
A child's heart cries
A family broken
No words spoken
Loveless emotion the token

A cycle of unresolved hurt
Repeat
Repeat
Repeat

It stops here
It stops now
No more asking why
Just
Teach Me How To Fly

Book Club Discussion Questions

1. What is the significance of the title? Would you have given the book a different title? If yes, what is your title?

2. What scene was the most pivotal for the book? How do you think the story would have changed had that scene not taken place?

3. What scene resonated most with you personally in either a positive or negative way? Why?

4. What surprised you the most about the book?

5. Did any of the characters remind you of yourself or someone you know? How?

6. What is motivating the actions of the characters in the story?

7. If you could smack any of the characters upside the head, who would it be and why?

8. Were there any moments where you disagreed with the choices of any of the characters? What would you have done differently?

9. What past influences are shaping the actions of the characters in the story?

10. Did you think the ending was appropriate? How would you have liked to have seen the ending go?

11. How have the characters changed by the end of the book?

12. Have any of YOUR views or thoughts changed after reading this book?

13. What do you think will happen next to the main characters?

14. What did you learn from, take away from, or get out of this book?

ABOUT THE AUTHOR

Alberta Lampkins is a passionate and dedicated advocate for children and adults. She has worked both in Child Protective Services and Adult Services. She is an Applied Suicide Intervention Skills trainer and currently works with military families. She is the Project Coordinator and contributing author of the book, *Messages to Our Children* and the founder of A.L. Savvy Publications.. She is an avid reader and the president of the Dazzling Divas Literary Club.

Alberta holds a B.A. and a M.A. Degree in Sociology from Fayetteville State University. She is the mother of two children, Alexis and Ahmad and the proud grandmother of her handsome grandson, Elijah. She is a native of Buffalo, New York, but currently resides in Tennessee with her husband CSM Albert Lampkins .

www.ingramcontent.com/pod-product-compliance
Lightning Source LLC
Chambersburg PA
CBHW070442120726
47910CB00003B/887